MW01065227

I Sing My
Psalm

Virginia:

God is concerned about
everything that concerns you!

Sheila P. Sanders

I Sing My Psalm

Psalm

— VOLUME 2 —

Shelia P. Sanders

Copyright © 2019 by Shelia P. Sanders.

Library of Congress Control Number:		2012913319
ISBN:	Hardcover	978-1-9845-7664-4
	Softcover	978-1-9845-7663-7
	eBook	978-1-9845-7662-0

All rights reserved. No part of this book may be reproduced or transmitted in any form or by any means, electronic or mechanical, including photocopying, recording, or by any information storage and retrieval system, without permission in writing from the copyright owner.

Any people depicted in stock imagery provided by Getty Images are models, and such images are being used for illustrative purposes only.
Certain stock imagery © Getty Images.

Print information available on the last page.

Rev. date: 01/11/2019

To order additional copies of this book, contact:
Xlibris
1-888-795-4274
www.Xlibris.com
Orders@Xlibris.com
786201

CONTENTS

Acknowledgements

First and foremost, I thank God, from whom all blessings flow, for the completion of this book. I give Him all honor and glory.

I thank my husband, Joseph S. Parker, Sr., for his encouragement and patience as I wrote. The Lord blessed us to be married while this book was still in its infancy stage.

Finally, I thank my daughter, Tracey McNeill, who has been unwavering in her help and support in the completion of this book.

Spoken Words

Spoken Words are to be a help, not a hindrance.
They are given so that the positive is manifested, not the negative.
Your words produced everything that was needed
in life, and we are to emulate you.
Lord, my prayer is that my words encourage someone;
that they build up and not tear down.

All of us need to be encouraged, from the one who seems to be
weighed down with trouble and strife to the one who appears to
be on top of the world. We want him to remain, not fall down.
Father, help us to push one another forward and
not pull each other down with our words.
We know that words have power because when
you said "Let there be", there was!

Our words should be carefully thought out before we say them.
Once they are spoken into the atmosphere they cannot be retrieved.
Help us to speak life!

Stained Glass

Father, I am like a window that You can see through.
There is nothing hidden; You see all that I am and all that I am not.
I don't want anything to mar the image You have of me.
I want Your view to be clear, not like stained glass.
I don't want to be pretty to look at, but not
having any spiritual substance.

I realize that I am not perfect, nor will I ever be,
but when my sin becomes evident, I want to repent
and be forgiven, not willingly continue in it.
Lord, stained glass is nice to look at, but the view is distorted.
My desire is to be perfectly clear.

We can't wipe the glass once in a while. Cleaning
is a habit that takes place consistently.
The window can't clean itself, neither can I clean up the
sin that creeps into my life. I must depend on You.
So Lord, I keep my hands and my heart lifted to You
for the thorough cleansing that only You can give.

Balanced Diet

We need to eat in the spirit just as we do in the natural.
Three meals a day is the normal regimen for our natural bodies.
However, we alter our diets as necessary.

Lord, I am blessed to know that I must partake of
the spiritual food to nourish my "inner man".
You are my spiritual food.
You are the bread of life and the living water
that I need to sustain my spirit.

Not having natural food will cause my body to die; just as
not having spiritual food will cause my spirit to die.
Thank You for making Yourself readily available to me.
I don't have to shop around for a bargain, I can just
come to the fountain that never runs dry.
Your word is my sustenance; it is the balanced
diet that my soul hungers for.
I need Your word to live because without You I don't have life.

There are times when I need more of You.
Times when my load seems to be too heavy, times
when my circumstances seem too much to bear.
These are the times when I saturate myself in Your
word, when I can't seem to get enough of You.
In the natural, we would call it overindulging, but
that word doesn't apply when I feed my spirit.
I can't ever get enough of You in me. I can
only yearn to become more like You.

Flat Line

Father, I don't want to complain about my peaks and valleys.
In life we will always have ups and downs.
When there is no change and everything remains
the same; completely straight with no deviations, we
have actually flat lined. Our lives are gone.

You never intended that we would have a trouble-free
existence. Our trials come to make us strong.
Because of Your grace and mercy our troubles don't last always.
How would we know that you are a burden
bearer if we never had any burdens?
Teach me to accept what You allow. Show me how to glean all that I
need from every situation so that I can continue to walk in Your ways.

Lord, I need You to be for me what I cannot be for myself.
You are the lifter up of my head.
I don't want to merely contemplate my state of being, I want to live
an abundant life which includes highs, lows, and moderate levels.
My desire is to savor each level of life to the
fullest and bring glory to You as I do it.

Container Garden

While looking at the beautiful flowers, I thought about Your people.
We are just like flowers and You plant us where we will do best.
Some of us thrive in a container garden, while others in an open field.

Container gardens fill many purposes.
They are ideally used in small spaces.
They can be moved to bear areas where their blossoms
bring transformation to their surroundings.

One thing to be noted is that flowers housed in a container don't
have to stay contained. They can be transplanted, just like us.
You have placed greatness in each of Your people and what
we have is not for ourselves, but for the body of Christ.
Lord, thank You for opening blind eyes and touching hearts to
know that You move Your flowers around for our own good.

Chimney Sweeper

When maintenance is needed in our homes, one of the
places we have inspected is the chimney because it is on
the roof and is susceptible to all types of weather.
Our bodies are Your dwelling places and we should always
inspect ourselves to see what may be in disrepair.
In our homes, we start at the top and in our
bodies we need to do the same thing.
We should begin with our minds. Have they been renewed?
Your words says "Let this mind be in you".
It is speaking about Your mind.
How often are we thinking our way, about our
stuff, and leaving You out completely?

Father, thank You for the instruction manual, which is the Bible. It
tells us everything we need to do to maintain Your dwelling place.
Every chance we get we need to do a spiritual chimney sweep
on our minds to make sure there are no obstructions.
We don't need anything in the way of receiving Your word
and hearing the Holy Spirit when He is directing us.

Help us to clean the clutter out of our minds
so that we can stay focused on You.
Sometimes our surroundings aggravate our
thoughts; sometimes it is people.
It is similar to being exposed to different types of weather.
We need to decide if damage is occurring or if the
experience is serving a Godly purpose.
Help us to be mindful that we have the task of
keeping Your dwelling in good condition.

We must also remember that You are the
landlord; our bodies don't belong to us.
We need to report any shortcomings, by way of repentance, and
allow You to do the work in us that we can't do within ourselves.

Tight Shoes

When our feet hurt, everything seems to hurt,
and we just can't function properly.
Most of the time we cause that pain by wearing tight shoes.
We are trying to wear the shoe that was meant for someone else.
We put the shoe on because we like the way it looks;
but can it endure the road we have to walk.

Our shoes have to handle all types of terrain.
Sometimes we'll walk a smooth path, but there will also be many
mountains to climb and plenty of valleys to go through.
We won't always walk in sunshine. Sometimes there
will be rain. Are the shoes waterproof?

Your word tells us that when we put on the whole armor of God
we should have the preparation of the gospel of peace on our feet.
We can't afford to be wearing tight shoes.
We must spread the gospel throughout the world,
willing to go wherever You lead us.

Compromising Position

Father, I thank You for Jesus.
Life throws us so many curve balls and each
one seems impossible to dodge.
Had it not been for saving grace there are many
times I would have been hit where it hurts.
I don't know how things happen so quickly, but one day everything
is well and the next day temptation is trying to take you down.

There are many times when the flesh wants to do
its own things, but flesh must be bought under
subjection and the Spirit must remain in control.
There should never be a situation that would cause me to be in a
compromising position, especially when I know Jesus died for my sins.
Thank You for keeping me, because I could never keep myself.
The enemy is always throwing things my way trying to seduce
me to succumb to his tricks, but Your word allows me to know
my enemy and remind him that he is already defeated.

Lord, I praise You for just who You are.
You created me, so You already know my frailties, however, You have
strengthened me to be able to overcome anything that comes my way.
Glory to Your name for making ways out of no way just for me.
Compromising is not part of my character, it's not what I do.
I will constantly keep my eyes on You while
going forward to my expected end.

Fire Insurance

We want to make sure our loved ones are taken care of in the event
of our death, so we make sure we get enough life insurance.
Life insurance is paid to survivors after we die.
My concern is how sure are we that we will
be taken care of after we die.
We need fire insurance to sidestep the fiery furnace.
Spiritual fire insurance pays off when we die.

Salvation is the only fire insurance that actually pays off.
It is not expensive at all, as a matter of fact it is free.
Many still don't have it because they want to
buy it. They believe the gospel is hype.
They say nothing is free.
Nobody gives their life for a world of strangers
Who uses blood to wash?
Let us say Oh, taste and see.

They say bread isn't life.
What is living water?
Who can be salt?
Let us say "try Jesus"!
He died, was buried and rose on the third day with all power.
He is the Son and God and He is coming back.
Accepting Jesus as your Savior and Lord is the guarantee
that the fiery furnace won't be your home.

The Tide

Every day the tide comes in and it goes out; it's just like clockwork.
The weather man tells us the exact time we can expect it.
We, however, should not be like the tide; in
and out. We ought to be constant.
Always abounding in Your Word.
Our praise should be continuous and our
walk should be forever in Your will.
Lord, I bless Your name for strengthening me
to maintain a right standing with You.
It is something I couldn't do myself.

I imagine that when the tide comes in, it brings with it some things
that are deposited in the sand that hadn't been there before.
I believe that when we walk away and come back, we bring
some additional things that You have to work on in us.
It's strange how we think we're missing out on some
things that were never meant for us in the first place.
How could be walk away from the best thing that ever happened to us?

Father, I so appreciate Your love and concern.
Thank You for accepting us back even though we don't deserve it.
The good thing is that no matter how far we
go, we can always come back home.
Truly, You are an awesome God. You never cease to amaze me.
The tide is a phenomenon in nature that must occur.
We, on the other hand, are not meant to go in and out.
Our behavior should be an enactment of Your Word
that says obedience is better than sacrifice.

Abandonment Issues

You said You would never leave me nor forsake me, so
I don't have to worry about abandonment issues.
You are all that is forever.
Too often we look to people and things to always
be there, but that will never happen.
Things won't last, nor will they ever make is eternally happy.

Relationships end, even when they begin with the best of intentions.
We start out as friends and end up every man for himself.
The relationship has been abandoned in favor of something new.

I delight myself in You, because You are the same today,
as You were yesterday and shall be forever more.
We tell one another I'm forever yours or we write
eternally yours in the closing of our letters when,
in reality, we are not in control; You are.
Our intentions may be in the right pace, but not
necessarily in sync with Your sovereign will.

Due Season

Many times we try to hurry You, but You operate outside of time.
Time was created for us. You transcend it,
You're not constrained by it.
Whatever we seek in life will be manifested in due season.

To everything there is a season and we are no exception.
There are times when our blessings seem to overtake
us. That's when we are in Your due season.
However, sometimes we are looking for a
blessing that seems to evade us.
It is then that we must exercise patience and wait on You.

Lord, I know that I will receive as I believe.
If I don't think it will come; if I can't see beyond
my right now, or if doubt supersedes my "yes Lord",
there is no need to look for manifestation.
Without a doubt, I know that You have great plans
for me. I just have to wait on my due season.
Although circumstances may attempt to dictate
my outcome, I will continue to stand firm.

Even when the world tells me it is impossible, I will still hold on.
No matter which way the wind blows, I
know that You control the wind.
I am expecting my due season to show up in perfect time.

Dream Deferred

Lord, it's amazing how we dream and make
plans for a future that You control.
I realize that there is no harm in having a vision,
because without a vision we perish.
However, the issue is, does our vision line up with Your will.
Father, help me to always be mindful to stay in
prayer concerning Your will for my life.

Help me to know that although I may have
aspirations and desires, the timing is Yours.
You may need to complete a work in me before I can proceed.
There may be some things that I am not yet ready to handle.
How about the experiences that I must have in
order to do or be what You desire for me?

What a blessing to know that sometimes my dream must be deferred
so that You can provide for me what I could never think or see.
Your thoughts are far beyond my thoughts;
and You desire the very best for me.
That's what a loving father does; gives the very best He has.

I may not always expect what You bring my
way, but I know it's what I need.
I may want You to move quicker, but I know You're always on time.
I don't always understand Your ways, but You told
me not to lean to my own understanding.
Hallelujah! My eyes have been opened to see that my dream
is deferred because you are perfecting it just for me.

Beyond the Sky

So often we hear the phrase "the sky's the limit", but it is a blessing to know we have hope in what's beyond the sky.

You are not confined by space or time. We must recognize that You are more than our finite minds can understand.

We can't get all of the sky in our eyes; nor can we completely see You for who You really are. You are all consuming, everything that is, was or shall be is in Your hands.

You are the light of the world and yet Your
light will shine through us, if we let it.

Although You have gone to prepare a place for us, You still remain here with us. Lord, You are beyond the sky while still keeping Your promise to never leave or forsake us.

You are definitely more than enough.

Awkward Silence

Lord, why do we sometimes think that when we
pray to You we must constantly talk?
Prayer isn't always one-sided. Not only do we
speak, sometimes You speak back.
We are of the mindset that we won't hear from
You right away, so we really don't listen.
Your small voice can't be heard through the crying and
pleading we're doing. If You speak we drown You out.

In Your Word You say "be still and know that I am God".
All parts of us should be still including our tongues.
It's okay for us to get before You with mute voices.
Sometimes we just need to bow down to Your omnipotence
and recognize You as the Almighty God You are.

We think of it as awkward silence when we are postured to pray
and there are no words, but words aren't always necessary.
This is when our hearts cry out and You hear us.
Then in the midst of the stillness we can hear from You

Answered Prayers

Lord, every prayer that I have prayed has been answered. However,
all of the answered prayers haven't come the way I wanted.
Sometimes what I prayed for seemed to take too long to
materialize; You answered in Your time instead of mine.
Other times my prayer, although, answered,
came in a totally different way.
I asked for what I thought was needed and You
gave what You knew was needed instead.

Many times You answered not now. These were those times
when You were preparing me to receive. When I asked, I really
wasn't ready to handle what I requested, and You knew that.
Then Lord, there were times when I asked and
You wanted to give me so much more.
I had put You in a box, actually limiting Your capabilities.
My finite mind couldn't imagine the blessings
You wanted to bestow upon me.

Father, You are God who hears and answers prayers.
You want to provide what is best for us, not just what we
request, because You know us better than we know ourselves.
I pray that we put ourselves in Your capable
hands and accept what You allow.

But God

Father, as I look back over my life I am reminded of so many
things that I have overcome; and I can only say But God!
There is nothing that I can brag about doing on my own,
because I have needed You every step of the way.
When I was at my lowest point, You bought me out.
When I seemed to be in a high place, You put me there.
When I lost my way, You were my compass
to point me in the right direction
When I succeeded, You blessed me with the success.

Lord, I couldn't make it without You. Thank you for
salvation because living this life without it is not living.
You alone have been the anchor to keep me grounded and You
have been my Rock when everything around me seemed to sink.
It has been relationship, not religion that sustained me. But God!
You are so much more than necessary, because
without You there is only death.

You have truly been a way out of no way
You have shown me how to maneuver
between a rock and a hard place
You have devoured every obstacle that stood in
the way of Your purpose for my life.
You have helped me see the impossible as possibility. But God!

Change in Perspective

Father, we don't always perceive things the way You intend us
to. A change in perspective can change our way of thinking.
Many times we see ourselves as small and incapable of being
and doing so many things that we freeze in place.
If we would hold on to Your word we would see that You made
us in Your image and we are fearfully and wonderfully made.

Lord, we often fret about our financial situations even
though we know You will supply all of our needs.
Your word tells us that we are the lender not the borrower, the head
and not the tail. We need to believe these things and act like it.
Words have power and that became evident when
You spoke everything into existence.
We need to speak out loud to ourselves. Let our words
break out into the atmosphere and declare what is.

Too often we look at situations and circumstances and
perceive things to be exactly as they appear. We need to
remember that faith is the evidence of things not seen.
Father, we must hold on to those things we are believing You for and
know, without doubting, that in Your time they shall manifest.
A slight change in perspective as to how we see ourselves will
enable us to rise up and overcome whatever is keeping us
from bringing forth the masterpiece that is within us all.

Changing Clothes

For many activities we don't have to change our clothing, but if
we intend to live for Christ we should be changing clothes.
We must take off what the world says is fashionable
and put on the whole armor of God.
We must put on the belt of truth, the breastplate of righteousness,
the gospel of peace, the shield of faith, the helmet of salvation
and the sword of the Spirit, which is the Word of God.
These are our war clothes, and each piece is essential.

Satan desires to stop us in our tracks by any
means necessary, so we must be prepared.
As in any war, you must know your enemy.
Sometimes we think we can take off pieces of the armor to slip
into places and fit in with people on a whim. But that's not so.
When we do that, it's called straddling the fence.
We must be prepared at all times, the enemy can
come in and destroy through a crack.

Father, don't let us get caught up in personalities. We must realize
we're fighting against principalities and powers, not people.
This warfare is all spiritual and the enemy
works through people just as You do.
That's why Your Word says "Let this mind be
in you which was also in Christ Jesus".
We must be transformed by the renewing of our minds.

Chilly Reception

Sometimes when I walk into a room the buzz
seems to simmer down to a mere whisper.
I'm conscience of it, but I continue walking anyway.
Lord, I just wonder why, what's going on, did something
happen? Then I look around to see who's there.
More often than not it turns out that the people who usually
give me those insincere greetings and fake "I'm happy to
see you smiles" are the ones who are in the room.
I haven't done anything to these people other than love
them with the love of Christ, so I have learned that their
reaction to my presence is not my problem it's theirs.

Your Word has taught me that my presence should make a difference.
People should not be comfortable doing certain things around me,
or any child of God, because we should be trying to walk like You.
This doesn't mean that we think we're better, because
that's not the case, it is just that when light shines darkness
has to leave...Why? Because it has been exposed.
Father, I know that we're in the world and not of the world so I'm
not obligated to participate in everything that the world does.

I love to be around people and sometimes they invite me
to come, and I show up and have a great time, but there
are other times when I'm not invited and those are the
times I shouldn't be there anyway, so it all works out.
But Father I wonder why people try to make
things so hard, it's not really necessary.

Then I remember that the enemy is always on his job.
He tries to mess with my mind and he tries to get a
reaction out of me. I don't react I make choices.
Thank You for reminding me that greater is He
that is in me than He that is in the world.

Cracked Pot

Father God, You are the Potter and I am the clay. I pray that when
You begin to make and mold me that I become a cracked pot.
Why? Because I know that some of You is in everything
You make and I want others to see You and not me.
I know there is no good thing in me, unless it is You.
Lord, a cracked pot can expose what's on the inside, it can
allow others to get a glimpse of Your righteousness.

Lord, I want Your light to shine in my life, help
me to live unapologetically for You.
I know it's not popular to go against the grain or to rub people
the wrong way, but right is right and wrong is wrong.
I choose to serve You with all that is within
me and I encourage others to look.
I can remember a time when I was timid in my walk, I had just begun
to know You; but now I know that boldness is the order of the day.

People need to see what You look like and my actions can show them.
Everybody is not going to church nor are they reading
the Bible, so how I act and treat them and others
may be the only peek of goodness they see.
Lord, Your Spirit is living on the inside of me and if
my pot is cracked just a little of Your light will shine
through; and with You, a little goes a long way.

Hidden Gems

Father, there are hidden gems in many of us. These gems are not
readily seen by others, but they are on the inside never the less.
Some have an anointing and the time to be displayed is not yet.
We never know what is housed in others. There is a tendency
to look at the outside appearance and make assumptions.

Lord, I don't want to judge a book by its cover nor do I
want to react to people the way others think I should.
I want to love everyone the way You love me.
The underdog seems to be the type I am
drawn to and I am grateful for that.
Usually, I am the one who is blessed because I am in their presence.

Thank you for leading me to the people I need to be with.
Likewise, I am thankful when You turn me
away from those I need to steer clear of.
You are an awesome God. You know the who, what, when
and where situations that should apply to us all.

Topped Trees

Lord, I looked out at the trees and saw how high they
reached into the sky and I began to wonder.
I wondered about people who have topped their trees because
they wanted them to stop growing up and start spreading out.
Then, I began to think about Your people who have decided to
cut short their vertical relationship in favor of a horizontal one.
So many have distanced themselves from You in order to be
with other people or to pursue things of interest to them.

We need an awakening Father. Help us to understand
that it's not about us and it never has been.
It's all about You.
Help us to see that You are the only one worth pursuing.
Although we say we're Holy, we display many holes in our
walk. People are always watching us, and we should be
showing them God in us, not how we yield to our flesh.
It is imperative that a turnaround takes place in our lives.

At times we may feel like joining in with the
world, thinking that we're only human.
We even come up with ways to justify our wants and desires;
in actuality, the justifications are tricks of the enemy.
I pray that we come to the realization that trying to
be like the world is not our goal, we should be urging
the world to give up their ways to follow You.
Let us showcase our obedience to You while
loving others as You have loved us.
Our relationship with You should not be like topped
trees, but it should continually grow upward.

Poor Visibility

There are many times when we can't see what's in front of
us. I'm speaking about the future that You have planned.
You have a predestined purpose for our lives
and sometimes we try to sidestep it.
Maybe we are afraid of appearing too different;
maybe we don't think we can do it;
It could be that it's not something we want to do; then there's
the possibility that we just can't stand to be blessed.

Father, help us to be obedient to the Spirit that You've
given to lead and guide us into all truth.
When we are obedient to You, we can expect blessings to overtake us.
It's easy to disallow ourselves to revel in Your blessings simply
because we don't think we deserve it. We really don't deserve it.
We need to understand that what You've put into
each of us is meant to be poured out.

You never intended that we would hold on
to the anointing that You gave us.
Some are anointed to preach, teach, sing, give, pray and
so much more. Each one of us has been gifted.
These gifts are not for us, but for the body of Christ.
When we don't go forward and do what we were
gifted to do, we cause others not to benefit.
Lord just because we have poor visibility and can't
see the end result, don't let us stifle the gifts.

Old Acquaintance

I ran into an old acquaintance the other day and I was delighted to
see him. We reminisced about the good times we had long ago.
Each of us had lived what seemed like a lifetime
since we had last seen one another.
Lord, in reality I had lived another life, because
I have since been born again.
He recognized the change in me and casually
mentioned I wasn't the same as he remembered.

Of course, he realized 30 years had passed and I had
matured; but that wasn't the only thing. I had been
transformed by the renewing of my mind.
God I thank You for not allowing me to conform to
the things of this world. Thank You for not allowing
me to be silent about my faith in You.
Your Word let's me know that if I am ashamed of You in this
sinful generation that You would be ashamed of me when You
return in the glory of Your Father with the holy angels.

My talk and my walk are completely different. It didn't have
anything to do with me, but everything to do with You.
Lord, it's wonderful to meet people from your past
and have them see what You have done.
I couldn't have done it myself; I loved the pleasures that life
offered me. In those days I pleased myself and enjoyed it.
Thank You for pulling me out of that life, I could have lost my soul!

What a blessing to be a walking, talking epistle,
allowing others to see You in me.
Lord please keep me in Your hands so I will
please You with all I say and do.
Although I am not perfect, I know that You are.
I desire to follow your perfect will for my life.

Tongue Tied

Lord, there are times when we should be quiet.
We can't always say everything we think.
We need to think before we speak. When words are released
into the air there's no way we can take them back.
Apologies are heard and accepted, but the
damage has already been done.
Too often we find ourselves feeling sorry for
ourselves because of the words we've spoken.

I pray that you help us to tame our tongues. Normally,
we use the phrase tongue tied when speaking
about a person who has trouble talking.
I use this phrase when indicating that the tongue needs to
be binded up. In other words we should tie it down.
Your word says that a man who can control his
tongue is able to control his entire body.
This indicates that taming the tongue is not easily done.

I want my tongue tied Lord. I never want to
purposely hurt someone because of what I say.
Let me always remember the power that words
have. They can build up or tear down.
They can make the difference in someone doing good
or doing bad; in persevering or giving up.
Father let my words make a positive difference.

Listening Ear

During my quiet times I sit back and think and
many times thoughts just come to my mind.
Father, I thought about how much time we spend talking and
how little time we are actually listening to what is being said.
Sometimes when people are talking to us all
they really require is a listening ear.
People don't always need our opinions or our two cents.
They just need to get something out of them.

Listening is an acquired skill because it doesn't just come naturally.
When we really tune in to someone, not only can we
hear what is said, we can also hear what is not said.
A wise person knows they should not keep everything on
the inside, we all have some things we need to release.
We choose to hold them in because they could be hurtful,
embarrassing, or shameful. Maybe we don't want to hear the backlash.
Whatever the case, I believe everyone needs someone who will listen.

Father, I pray that You would bridle my
tongue and give me a listening ear.

Downsizing is Prohibited

All of us are created in Your image even though
You have made each of us unique.
You never intended for us to recreate ourselves to
our own specifications because then we wouldn't
measure up to Your master plan.
We would try to be like someone else, but You made no
two alike; even twins have different fingerprints.

It was never your intention that we downplay what
You have given us. It is neither necessary nor feasible
to conceal our abilities or our weaknesses.
When we can we should do and when we can't
we should know our limitations.
Lord, You can overcome any limitation. Sometimes we must
yield to the one You have prepared to do a certain thing.
This is called staying in our lanes.

You have given each of us gifts and talents
that should be used for Your glory.
We must stop reducing what You've put in us
so that others can feel comfortable.
People may not always give their nod of approval to
everything we say or do, and that's alright.
They may not understand the reasons why because
You don't reveal the same things to everybody.
We are not all at the same level in our relationship with You.
Actually, some people may not have a relationship
with You at all, they might just be "religious".

Lord, help us to strive to be all we can be in You.
Don't let us downsize ourselves.
Downsizing is prohibited because everything
You've given us is not just for ourselves.
We are blessed to be a blessing to others.
We should be about building the kingdom up
There is room for all of us, after all we really are the
bricks that should be fitly joined together.

I Am Evidence

Lord God, I am grateful for every testimony I hear, every
sermon I hear and every Bible verse I read, but I know for
myself that You are God and besides You there is no other.
I know that You are a miracle worker, a way out of no
way, a bridge over troubled water, a doctor, a lawyer, and
whatever anybody needs You to be for any reason.
All I have to do is look back over my life and
see where You've bought me from.
The evidence is in the struggles I've gone through.
To put it another way, I am evidence!

Testimonies are wonderful, but I am able to look at my own life and
know that You were working at all times through every day of my life.
So many times I thought I wouldn't make it. So much was being
thrown my way, I thought I couldn't take it, but You sustained me!!
Father, You strengthened me to be able to go on. I am evidence
that we can do all things through Christ which strengthens us.

I remember when I thought there was no way I
could achieve accomplishments that You allowed
to manifest in my life.....I am evidence.
There were times when I felt at my lowest, when it seemed like life
had been snatched from me; but You let me live....I am evidence.
There were also so many joys You blessed me to see and
experience that were beyond my wildest dreams. Only
You could bring them to pass.....I am evidence

Father, my voice will not be silent about who You are,
nor can I live my life without placing You first in it.
I have my own story to tell about how great You are.
There is nothing and no one who can be compared to You.
You are the creator of everything.
You are God, who never changes; You are
the one who makes changes.

Kingdom Encounter

I have managed to go through some hard things somehow.
I have also had some experiences that needed to
be suppressed for someone else's benefit.
But, it wasn't until You made a move in my life that showed me
exactly who You were that I understood a kingdom encounter.
Serving You comes with persecutions and mistreatment
sometimes. It's not always sweet, but You didn't say it would be.

Leaning and trusting in You have shown
me there is victory in despair.
It doesn't matter what comes my way, I know that
the enemy has already been defeated.
I have felt the sting from a smile and have recognized insincere
intentions only because You brought them to my attention.
There is a reason for everything that You allow.

Sometimes I have to just be still and know that You are God.
In Your infinite wisdom, You will handle everything that
presents itself, whether for my good or my detriment.
I love You Lord, and the joy of You is my strength.
Continue to have Your way in my life. Lead
and guide me as You see fit.

Don't Delay

I remember the old saying "don't put off until tomorrow
what you can do today." I thought how appropriately this
saying applies to accepting the gift of salvation.
Your Word lets us know that today is the day of
salvation and so many of us refuse to accept it.
We have all kinds of excuses.
Sometimes we say that we have to get ourselves
together before we can come to You.
We can't get ourselves together; it's impossible.
You are the only one who can do that.

Other times we say that we will come to You when we're older.
Your Word says to suffer the little children.
Why do we insist on living in darkness when
You can provide a marvelous light?
What is so great about gaining the whole world and losing our souls?

Then, there are those who don't believe they can be forgiven.
Lord, I pray that everyone comes into the knowledge
that Jesus died for the sins of the world.
He laid down His life for all sins; past, present and future.
Not only that, but He picked it up again. He lives!!!!!

Salvation is available, accept it and live. Don't Delay

Perfect Ending

Father, I am grateful for the life You have given me, for every experience You have allowed me to have, for every place You have allowed me to go and for every person You have put in my path.

You have taken me through some hard times and brought me to some wonderful times. However, at no time did you leave me. Lord, You have shown me myself on numerous occasions. You have allowed me to see the real deal, even when I was in denial.

It wasn't done to discourage me, but to encourage me
to do better. You have shown me how to push past
negativity until I get to the thing You put in me.
You put a gift within me, You put purpose within me, and You
enabled me to tap into them so that You could be glorified.

Lord God, thank You for loving me. Thank You for rescuing me
from me. It's always the flesh trying to overtake the Spirit.
My only desire is to have a perfect ending.
I long to be ready when You come.

Reciprocal Love

We often settle into a give and take relationship with
You Lord, but that's not the way it should be.
You love us unconditionally and You give what is best
for us; however we don't always give back.
We allow You to give while we just take;
that's not really a relationship at all.
You said in Your Word that we should love You with all
of our heart and all of our soul and all of our mind.

Father, You want reciprocal love. Since nothing can
separate us from Your love, we shouldn't be so quick to
step backwards when things don't go our way.
What we really do is turn to idols. Idols are whatever
has more priority in our lives than You do.
We have a tendency to love things, positions, titles, and money.
Our attention is focused on our houses, cars, jobs and bank
accounts. Don't we realize that You gave us these things?

Lord, You have shown us what love is really
like and we should follow Your lead.
Help us to get rid of the selfish attitude we sometimes have.
It's not about us, but it's all about You.
You are the creator and we are Your creation.

Remind us that the same things we do automatically
in a natural relationship should also be how we
respond in our relationship with You.
I pray that we grow in our love relationship,
that we become more like You.
We haven't arrived yet, but Father we're striving.

Holding On

Lord, You've brought me a mighty long way. You've
kept me when I couldn't see my way clear.
I didn't think about my next step and I didn't
want to ponder on my future.
All I knew was that I was still here and he wasn't.
Father, You enabled me to go on anyhow. You encouraged
me and carried me and now I am strengthened
for having gone through the experience.

I learned how to be alone without being lonely.
I accepted my single state of mind and began
to stop thinking of myself as coupled.
After some years, I began to enjoy my new way of
life; I could give more of myself to You.
I was able to serve without reservations, after all, I no longer had
to consider anyone else. All of me was now available for your use.

And then it happened; I was being noticed and pursued.
I was a little uncomfortable, but yet quite pleased. I recognized
that I enjoyed the attention and was happy to have the company.
Little by little bits and pieces of my time
seemed to be slipping away from me.
Lord, I wasn't really focused on eternal things,
I was focusing on my calendar.

Although I spent quality time with You, it wasn't the same as before.
I wanted to appease the pursuer somewhat,
and somewhere I lost some of me.
Father, You have shown me facets of myself that I didn't know existed.
You opened up areas in the inner part of me that
had never been exposed to me before.

I intend to hold on to all that I now know I am. All of
these things are an expression of my uniqueness.
Continue to speak to me and lead me in the ways I should go.
There are still some unchartered areas within me that I must explore.
Holding on is my new mantra, it's the song in my
heart. I will not forsake the glimpse of my possibility
in order to become part of a couple.

Tired Places

Lord, You said to watch as well as pray and
I thank You for Your Word.
I not only need to watch my surroundings,
but I need to watch myself.
Every area in my life hasn't received the rest of God, so I need
to recognize the tired places; the broken areas in my life.

The enemy comes to attack my brokenness and if I'm too
busy basking in my resting place I'll be blindsided.
He's always trying to distract me. He wants to get a
reaction out of me, but Your Word orders my steps and
doesn't allow me to react. Instead, I make decisions.

I have decided to follow You.
You alone know my beginning as well as my end.
In my weakness it is You who makes me strong.
I can do all things through Christ which strengthens me.

Unborn Potential

Father, when You created us, You filled us with so many things. You put into us what we would need and what we could share with others. In Your infinite wisdom, You didn't give us all the same things, but you gave as You desired.
It's amazing how so many people live a full life and others hardly live at all. They never expose all of the possibilities that are on the inside of them.

Sometimes it is fear that makes people keep their unborn potential under lock and key.
Other times it's complacency; they just want to keep things the way they've always been. They have no need or desire to explore what could be.
Oftentimes, it is laziness, they don't want to sharpen the skills they have because it would mean they would have to do some work.
Lord, don't let us hold on what was meant to be set free.

Why do we insist on staying pregnant with what could be instead of giving birth to what should be?
Father, You are a master craftsman. You didn't make anything that wasn't good. Open our eyes to the unborn potential you placed in us to be released in its season.
Let Your will be done in us and through us.

I'm Enough

Father God, I thank You for letting me know
I am fearfully and wonderfully made.
When You created me You gave me all that I
needed to function the way You intended.
That doesn't mean that I shouldn't strive to better myself, to learn
and to grow, but it does mean that I should thrive in what I have.
I'm grateful for all that You deposited within
me, not just me, but in all of us.
You gave each person exactly what You wanted them to have.

It's our job to know our gifts and talents, and then work in them.
The kingdom needs exactly what we have to give.
Each of us has a gift that we can't stifle. We can't hold
back what is trying to come forth to give You glory.
We can't be like anyone else, we just have to use what we've
been given and know that it's our kingdom work.

I may not be in the limelight, but my light can still shine.
I may not receive applause, but You still say well done.
At times I may not be appreciated by others, but I do
everything as unto the Lord so it doesn't matter.
Sometimes I may feel that I'm inadequate when I look at all
the greatness around me, but I can't be lead by my feelings.
I give You praise because I know that I'm enough.

Perfectly Imperfect

Everything You created was good, but because of
the fall in the Garden, man has a sin nature.
It's because of this that we are born in sin and shaped in iniquity.
Therefore, we know that we are not without some faults.
There are things within us that are perfectly
imperfect and that was Your decision.

At no time should we consider ourselves to be flawless.
We have to recognize that You alone are perfect.
Your Word tells us to let Your mind be in us;
thereby changing the way we think.
We should always strive to be like You, but understand
that we will be striving until You come back.

Lord, don't let us talk about or look down on anybody,
because there is room for improvement in all of us.
Help us to recognize what we need to work on within
ourselves so that we can be all that You intended.
Our imperfections should keep us on our
knees yielding ourselves to Your will.

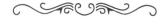

Middle Season

Why do we have a hard time believing what
You said. If You said it, it shall be so.
Many times, we question You.
We have to learn how to wait. The time between what
You said and what You do is the middle season.
Waiting is the hardest part, but it's the part
that makes all the difference.

Too often we jump the gun by moving forward
when You haven't given us the go ahead.
Sometimes we lag behind, when we should have moved
already, not realizing that You have perfect timing.
Lord, You may tell us what will be, but it will
happen in Your time, not ours.
Help us to know the difference.

The middle season is a time when the enemy
tries to mess with our minds.
He tries to put doubt in us. He works the same as he always has
and we must remember that he's a liar and the father of lies.
Help us to hold on even when it looks hopeless.
After all, we walk by faith and not by sight.

Old Flower

It's wonderful to be young and vibrant, but it's such a blessing
to be old and useful, still working for the kingdom.
Father, let me be an old flower in the garden of life. I want to
be a perennial, popping up every year to bring You glory.
Sometimes it is easy to become complacent and stagnate, but
this happens when we decide not to put forth any effort.
We decide to wither away, thinking that is our last duty in life;
however, Your Word tells us to work until our days are done.
We may not do what we've done in the past, but we work nevertheless.

Every time my eyes are closed doesn't mean I'm
sleeping, I am just meditating on Your Word.
Every time I wave my hand, it's not because I'm
leaving, I am just giving You praise.
I'm just like the old adage "every shut eye ain't
sleep and every goodbye ain't gone".
I take this life seriously and I truly believe that my last
days are my better days, so I want to live like it.

Yes, my hair has changed colors. It shows my
maturity and I love how the silver sparkles.
My steps are a little slower, it's only because I choose
to linger a little longer to enjoy where I am.
My words may not come as fast as they used to, it's
because I think about them before I let them flow.
Lord God, old flowers are still beautiful and I'm
grateful that you enjoy the fragrance.

Strange Land

Father, we are living in a strange land. Everything
about the world we currently live in is abnormal.
The world has become exactly what Your Word said it
would be. People call right wrong and wrong right. They
have become lovers of themselves, they are lovers of pleasure
rather than lovers of God and they despise good.
The Word says these are perilous times.

We have been caught up in the things of the world and
have let the eternal things fall by the wayside.
Lord help us to see You and not look to
people or things for fulfillment.
Your Word says that if we seek You first all
others things would be added to us.
We must not really believe what You say,
otherwise our actions would be different.

Lord, help us to know that Your Word is true and that we shouldn't
get comfortable living in this world, because this is not our home.
It is stranger that we have begun to act like the world
instead of being the example for the world to follow.
We say we don't want to rock the boat, but we don't realize that
the boat has already capsized, and the reason is compromise.

I pray that we repent and make a change while there is still time.
One thing is certain, You are a merciful God and I ask
that you please have mercy on us in Jesus' name.

Dirty Hands

Oh, how I love giving You praise and worship. I bow
down to Your glory and Your omniscience.
Father, as I raise my arms up high I hope filth is not what You see.
I don't want to wave dirty hands in Your face because
I haven't done what I was called to do.
Lord, I don't want the blood of those I failed
to witness to be on my hands.

You told us to go into the world to tell people of You; to take
the gospel to them and to teach them what we have learned.
I don't want to be guilty of only selecting certain
people to tell of Your goodness and Your grace.
I don't want to find myself ashamed of sharing You with anyone.
Lord, You are not a respector of persons. Your love is extended to
everyone, nobody is excluded and my goal is be more like You.

Father, our assignment is to GO, so why are some of
us standing still. Why are we frozen in place.
You haven't given us the spirit of fear, but of
power, and of love and of a sound mind.
Lord, we already have within us what we need to obey Your word.
We have the power to carry out our assignment, the
love to want to see it accomplished and the mind
to choose to do it; so what's the problem?

Dirty hands should be a fallacy with us something that
shouldn't even be mentioned or thought about. Our hands
are the ones You use to enhance the lives of others.
Our hands are to serve You and others, and should
not be filled with hypocritical intentions.
Father forgive us for our slothfulness; forgive us for pretending
we have it all together when in actuality our lifted hands
show You we have not helped to bring others to You.

Work Out

I can remember hearing older people talk about "working out their soul's salvation." The more I think about that phrase I realize we should be saying the same thing. We are busy with a work out, but it's for our physical bodies. Certainly we need to be physically fit; however, we also need to be spiritually fit.

Lord, I pray that I put the first thing first. My concern should be about eternal things, so my focus should not be on the things of this world. I want my body to be in good shape so that I can serve You better, but I don't want to be so consumed with my work out that I neglect my time with You.

My desire, like so many others, is to get to the gym three times a week. I don't always succeed, but I make an attempt. When I don't make it I sometimes say, "life happens". Well, if the truth be told, without You I wouldn't have life.

Father, there should never be a day that goes by when I don't spend time with You. I need to be in Your Word, on a daily basis, to get direction for living my life. You are the one who causes my heart to beat, my mind to function, my limbs to move and my mouth to speak. I must bow down to Your omnipotence every chance I get.

Lord, it's only by Your grace and mercy that I breathe so I don't ever
want to get so centered on my activities that I fail to place You first.
Thank You for already knowing my heart
and making a difference in me.
I will worship You and give You all the glory
as I work out my soul's salvation.

Dig Deep

My Father, there are times when You speak to my situation
right away. As I read Your Word a scripture will become
illuminated because it is just what I need at that time.
However, there are other times when I have to dig
deep to receive the revelations You have for me.
I am so thankful for the nuggets You pass my way because I no
longer have to struggle for solutions. You bless me with what I need.

Lord, it's evident that You are concerned about everything that
concerns me, no matter how insignificant it may seem to others.
You love me beyond measure.
I know, without a doubt, that when I dig through the
Bible I will find exactly what I need because You said seek
and I will find, knock and the door will be opened.
All of my trust is in You.

We sometimes act as if it's a mystery to hear from You, but You
have already given us the answers to our questions in Your Word.

Wearing Masks

Are we really sure that the person we see is
the same person we think we know?
Many people are wearing masks because they
don't want to expose who they really are.
Lord, why do we allow our past, or maybe our present
state, dictate how we present ourselves to others?
Most of the time there is negativity that we're trying to
hide, but sometimes we try to hide what's positive.

We end up wearing masks because we are overly concerned
about what people will say or what they will think.
The real question is how we really feel
about ourselves. Who do we see?
We should recognize that transparency is freeing.
When "what you see is what you get" is our mantra,
think of the good that can come out of that.

If we live for Christ and we are obedient to His Word,
then Christ will be reflected in our lives.
People won't really see us, but the Christ that is
in us. He is the light that will shine.
Everybody has something they want to keep to themselves.
Nobody wants everything about them exposed.
There are no perfect people.

If negativity causes us to wear masks, we need to repent and
believe that God has forgiven us, then take the masks off.
If positivity causes us to wear masks, we need to use everything
God has given us; it's not just for us, but for the Body of Christ.
Lord, don't allow us to let our gifts and talents lay dormant. We
were blessed to be a blessing and You gave as You saw fit.

Thrown Away

Things are thrown away when they are of no more
use. They are broken and can't be mended.
We are Your creation and we are made in Your image, so
we should never feel like we have been thrown away.
We should never walk over people as if they
Are trash, are of no use or invaluable.
All of us were created in Your image.

You are love and there is nothing that can separate us from Your love.
Lord, You show us unconditional love everyday.
We should try to love one another in the same way You love us.
We need to remember that we cannot judge others lest we be judged.
However, strange things are happening in the land.

I hear on the news and read in the paper that
people are being thrown away.
Babies are aborted, children are killed by parents and parents are
killed by children; drugs are leaving people dead in the streets.
There is nothing natural about the things that are taking place now.
Your Word says this is just the beginning of sorrow
Things, not people, should be thrown away.

Fake News

The phrase "fake news" has become very popular lately
and in my mind either it is news or it is not.
News is defined as reported information, however, being
reported doesn't necessarily make it true. Fake news
would indicate that it hasn't even been reported.
Lord it seems that this type of play on words is exactly what the
enemy uses to confuse people when it comes to Your word.

One thing is for sure, Your word is truth, not to be confused
with factual information, because sometimes the facts, as
we know them, are very different from Your truth.
The facts show that a child cannot be conceived without intercourse;
The facts show that a woman in her nineties
is past childbearing age; and
The facts show that a donkey cannot talk
But the truth is all of these things happened.
It's not natural; it's supernatural.

We have to concern ourselves with more truth and less news.
Jesus is the way, truth and the life.
Father, you have given Your Son to die for the sins of
the world. There's no greater love than that.
It behooves us to prepare ourselves to be ready
for His return and that's the truth.

Uncommon Solution

Whenever things don't go our way, or when we have a
problem, we pray for You to solve our dilemma.
We usually have thoughts of how everything should work out.
We even ask You to solve things according to our vision.
We see the end result as only a finite mind can envision it.
What we don't take into consideration is that You are God who
is able to produce possibilities that we aren't capable of seeing.

In Your infinite wisdom, You will bring
about an uncommon solution.
You aren't going to do an ordinary thing
because You are an extraordinary God.
Not only will You bring about amazing results, You
will bring results that only You could bring.
People will say "Look at God" because they know we
don't have it in us to bring about a perfect end.
You will get the glory because all glory belongs to You.

Lord, I remain in awe of You because You do everything
with excellence and nothing about You is average.
You pour out overflowing blessings, so that
our expectations are always exceeded.
Although it sounds like a cliché, You may not come
when I want You to, but You're always on time.
Additionally, You may not do exactly what I
ask, but You constantly blow my mind.

Position Ourselves

Father, You called us out. You set us apart for Your
use, so it is up to us to position ourselves.
We shouldn't be in the places You called us out of, nor should
we be with the people You told us to distance ourselves from.
The fact is, we were delivered from some things, people
and places and it doesn't make any sense to travel
backward when You're trying to take us forward.
Why would we help temptation to overtake us; that's absurd.

Lord, our strength is in You, so we need to stay close.
Help us to yield ourselves to Your will and not to our flesh. Because
if the truth were told, we would still be doing everything we wanted.
We think that we came to You, but the reality is that
we were chosen; that alone should be enough to make
us position ourselves where You need us to be.

We are of no use if we aren't willing to be soldiers in Your army.
You need bold soldiers, who are willing to make sacrifices.
This is spiritual warfare, not hiding go seek.
Thank You for giving us opportunities to step back and look at
ourselves and then make adjustments to be completely Yours.
Thank You for helping us to recognize that we don't belong to
ourselves, but we're Your creations chosen specifically for Your use.

Wake Up

This is not a dream, this is reality.
And yet I still need to wake up.
What is going on in my community, in my city, in my country?
What is happening to the family, the government and the people?
Things I never thought I would see, nor do I want to see.

Father, Your Word makes things plain to us.
You said there would come a time when people
would be lovers of themselves.
You said we would call wrong right and right wrong.
You said there would be wars and rumors of wars.
You also said we would only tell the seasons
by the budding of the trees.

Lord, God You said mothers would be against daughters.
You said daughters would be against mothers
You said fathers would be against sons.
You also said sons would be against fathers.
But the end is not yet.

These are definitely the end times and the church
needs to rise up in order to wake up the people.
Your Word also tells us there is a time for all things.
There is a time to be silent, but this isn't that time.
The church needs to speak out against what is wrong.

Down Payment

Father, I get so excited just thinking about meeting You
face to face because then I would be in heaven. I think
about how You've given us a down payment on heaven.
The Bible describes it in terms I could never imagine.
It is far more than anything I have dreamed of,
heard of or could conceive of ever seeing.
The down payment You gave to me is the Holy
Spirit, and He helps me to live here on earth until
that glorious day when You call me home.

Lord, I can't imagine life without the Holy Spirit. I
don't know how I would be able to function.
He orders my steps, directs my path, speaks to my heart
and generally helps me to know what to do next.
He urges me to do those things that are in Your will and
He also lets me know when I step outside of Your will.
Lord, when I think about what You've done for me I can't help put
give You praise. The down payment of the Holy Spirit in my life is
so wonderful that I shiver at the thought of eternal life in Heaven.

I have no doubt in my mind about the depth of Your love for me.
I can't express it in mere words and my mind can't fathom
all the facets of Your love, but Lord God I'm grateful.
As undeserving as I am, You love me. In
spite of my faults You still love me.
Father, my life is in Your hands; use it as You have
purposed and know that I love You too.

Uniquely Made

Truly blessed is how I see myself. I am one of
a kind and I cannot be duplicated.
Lord I thank You that I am uniquely made and the
incredible thing is that everyone else is also.
You didn't make any of us alike. We all have
something different to offer the world.
We are just as individual as snowflakes.

As I look around I see so many people trying to
imitate others. What is the reason for that?
Be uniquely you is what I say. The differences
in us makes us who we are
When we alter our looks to appear as someone else what
we're really saying is what You made is not good enough.
When we take on someone else's personality we
are really throwing away what You put in us. We
don't think our individuality is sufficient.

Father, You gave each of us what You wanted us to have.
Different is still good whether we see it that way or not.
You look at our hearts and not our outside appearance.
We need to get our hearts right and everything else will fall into place.

Knee Deep

Father God, I thought about how blessed I am to be saved.
You offered salvation and I accepted and it's
the best gift I've ever received.
There's nothing I can do to repay You. All I
can do is believe and obey Your word.
I'm so in awe of You that I want to do more than get knee
deep in Your word, I want to saturate myself in it.

You said that obedience is better than sacrifice, so I must obey.
In order to obey I have to study to be able to rightly divide the word.
Father, I have to understand exactly what You're saying to me.
I have to be taught and I have to depend on the Holy
Ghost to reveal to me what I need to know.

Lord I want to continue to grow in You. I want to constantly
increase and mature on this Christian journey.
I never want to get to a place where I think I know
enough because You said to remain teachable.
I am keeping my spiritual eyes and ears open to
glean from the lessons You set before me.

Sweet Words

Heavenly Father, when You gave us Your Word, You made it
plain and when we give it to others we need to be plain as well.
You never intended that we sugarcoat Your
Word because You want it to help us.
Why is it that so many dance around the true
meaning in order to make it sound good?
Sweet Words can't order our steps.

So often Your Word is softened when the
preacher doesn't want to offend.
But, Your Word is quick and powerful,
sharper than any two-edged sword.
It should be used for doctrine, for reproof, for
correction, and instruction in righteousness.
Rather than twisting the Word, we should
use it for its intended purpose.

Help us realize that we cannot lead people astray
by giving them a distorted Word.
When we should be preaching the Gospel but we're talking about
ourselves, this is when E.G.O. kicks in. We are easing God out.
We may have the platform, we may be the one who is
seen, but it's not about us; its's all about You.
Lord, please deliver us from egotistical behavior.

Dwelling Places

Lord, You have given us freewill.
We're free to choose what to do and how to do it.
Oftentimes, our choices stunt our growth.

We choose to dwell in places of malcontent.
We are never satisfied with what we have.
We are always trying to get what someone else has.
We never exercise the abilities You have placed in us, because
we are always striving to be like the next person.

We choose to dwell in lonely places.
Constantly isolating ourselves, then complaining
that people never seek us out.
Using social media to mix and mingle
instead of accepting the invitation.

We choose to dwell in uncertainty.
We will not take a forward step because
we are not sure of the outcome.
We wonder what others will think.

We choose to dwell in fear.
Always afraid that our best effort isn't good enough.
We worry that others won't accept us as we are.

Lord, I choose to dwell in You.
In You, all things are working for my good.
In You, there is no failure.

Artificial Boundaries

Many times we hold up our own blessings. We
decide what You can and cannot do.
We only expect to receive certain things and then
we believe they can only come one way.
Depending on our finite minds to conceive what we can have
or what we can do causes us to build artificial boundaries.
In essence, we are putting You in a box.
You are a mighty big God who can do impossible things;
but we think small so we live beneath our privilege.

Artificial boundaries cause us not to stretch
forth to reach our full potential.
We settle for average and forego the greatness that is within us.
I pray for release.
Father, release me from feelings of inadequacy.
Release me from always walking behind, when in
fact, sometimes You intend that I lead.

I pray for an awakening.
Awaken the creativity within me that desires to come forth.
Awaken my desire to go for the things I have always wanted
to do instead of stopping short because of naysayers.
Lord, I see that I have put up artificial boundaries;
however, I gratefully recognize that I must also tear
them down in order to allow You to move.

No Shortcuts

There are no shortcuts to heaven, and rightly so, because
You have given us the instructions in the Bible.
It doesn't matter what we think might work, or what we
have been told by others there is still only one way.
Jesus is the way, He's the truth and He's life. As a matter of
fact, He's the door to heaven. There is no other way.

Lord, I believe this with all of my heart. I know people
who believe differently, but that doesn't affect my
belief at all and it doesn't change what You said.
We have to be born again. We have to be
transformed by the renewing of our minds.
We often hear about people who are good and do good
things, but if they haven't been born again, it doesn't
matter how good they are they won't enter heaven.

Father, I pray that we study Your word for ourselves. I pray
that we don't just accept what people tell us as gospel.
Sometimes people don't get it right. People will
embellish the Word to make it sound better or take
something away to make it more acceptable.
We need it just the way it has been given.
I pray that we have the desire to read Your word
and that You give us the understanding we need to
live for You, because there are no shortcuts.

So often I may ask You to make a way for me to do something,
but have I even looked around to see what I could do?
Father, You have already placed so many things within
reach just waiting for the opportunity to be used, and I
haven't recognized the potential that is in them.
It is always easier to ask and receive than
it is to come up with a solution.
Lord, I don't want to become lazy, I want
to work for the things I want.

I want to use the mind You have given me to work things
out. The easy way out is not always the better way.
You have placed everything we need within us, so I want
to call some things out to use whenever necessary.
Some things within reach are being used in other capacities,
but that doesn't mean they can't do double duty.

I think about the widow and the oil and realized that
although the vessels in her house either were empty or held
other things, they were still capable of holding oil.
Father God, I need to apply that same analogy to my life.
Thank You for lifting the scales from my eyes so I can
see the various uses for things within my reach.

Morning Stretch

Father, I want to do more than move my
body during my morning stretch.
I want my heart to stretch out to You.
It is about getting in touch with You so my day can begin.
I need Your guidance so I must stretch out
to You in order to receive it.

I have to wait in holy anticipation for You to speak to me.
Lord, speak by any means necessary to order my steps.
I know that You have the final say in my day; my plans
may not be what You have planned for me.
You can see the end of my day before it has even begun.

Maybe I need to show up in someone's life today or give to a need.
I want to do whatever You require of me.
I take my morning stretch seriously because it is the spiritual
meeting I have before I can do the work I am called to do.
Everyday I want to stretch to the limits to
work out my soul's salvation.

Stray Hairs

Lord, when it seems that everything is going well,
something unexpected comes to shake things up a bit.
I compare it to getting caught in a windstorm without any protection
and my hairdo is completely gone. Stray hairs are all over the place.
Spiritual warfare is what is actually happening.
These stray hairs come riding on the waves
of adversity, trying to trip me up.
The enemy knows he only has a short time, so he wants to
do as much damage as possible to the Body of Christ.

His desire is to make me forget that greater is He
who is in me than he who is in the world.
He wants to get a reaction, hoping that I will
try to do what You have already done.
Your word lets us know that Satan is already defeated.
Nevertheless, the enemy continues to throw darts our way.

The enemy stays on his job, but we sometimes let our guard down.
We complain about things that happen instead
of trying to see the bigger picture.
Nothing happens by chance, everything has a reason. We should
think about what we can learn from the things that happen to us.
Instead of turning a deaf ear to the small talk, we allow
negativity to creep into relationships based on gossip.
We already know the enemy wants to divide
us; however, united we stand.

We should recognize the adversary for who he is.
We shouldn't help him bring us down.
Father, remind us that we will have trouble and storms
are going to come, but they only come to make us
stronger, not to make us give in or give up.
When everything seems to be going well, enjoy it, but know that
"stray hairs" will show up when least expected, but they won't stay.
Our good days always outweigh our bad.

Safe Haven

Father, we have a safe haven in You.
There is no place we can go and nobody we can turn to
who can provide the protection that only You can give.
Lord, sometimes we need protection from ourselves
because of the sin nature that is within.
We cannot blame the enemy for everything
because some blame belongs to us.

Lord, I am so thankful to have a safe haven in You.
Without You I would not have anywhere to
turn. You are my strong tower.
As I read Your Word, You say that "a thousand shall
fall at my side and ten thousand at my right hand; but
it shall not come near me." How awesome is that?
You are my protection. Lord I bow down to
Your omnipotence. You are my God.
There is no love that surpasses the love You have for me.

Lord, I am in awe of You. No matter what my
need is You are able to provide it.
I come to You for all things and all of my trust is in You.
I lean on You Lord, because You are my everything.
You won't sway or turn around.
Father, You are always the same. What You do for one You
will do for another. You are no respecter of persons.
You love me in spite of me. I don't deserve it
and yet You shower me with blessings.
Thank You for salvation. Thank You for saving grace.

Called Out

Heavenly Father, although we are in the world we
are not of the world. We are the called out.
We are the ones You will use for Your purposes.
You desire that we be salt so we can season all that is in the
world. Without our saltiness we can't do anything.
We should let others see You in us. We should also be
light because when light appears darkness has to flee.

Lord, help us to walk circumspectly so that
the enemy can not deceive us.
We must be watchful and vigilant because
Satan is always trying to trip us up.
He stays on his job because he knows his days are numbered.
We must do the same so we can be ready whenever You come for us.

Being called out is a privilege that should not be taken lightly.
You desire that we spend eternity with You, but everybody won't.
You have given us freewill so our choices determine our eternal home.
Hell was never created for us, but it has enlarged
itself to accommodate those who will enter in.
If the called out would actually come out
this would not be an issue for us.
We must be on our jobs to lead others to You.

Window Shopping

What makes us skim through Your Word
instead of reading and studying it?
In it You tell us to study to show ourselves approved unto You.
It seems as if we're just window shopping, looking for
something of interest, not anything to live by.
You gave us all of the word for our benefit, not bits and pieces of it.
We have to eat the whole roll, not just bite
pieces that seem good to us.
Lord, Your Word wasn't meant to be looked at. It
was given to us so we could live for You.
It is our basic instructions before leaving earth.

We really don't have the option of checking
things out first to see if we want it.
All of it is for us and it's meant to make us more Christ-like.
You didn't just give us a story to read, but you
gave us a way to live until You return.
You expect us to be obedient to Your word and unless
we read it we won't know what You're saying to us.

Father, continue to do a work on the inside
of us that shows up on the outside.
You are definitely a longsuffering God; You constantly show us that.
No matter how much or how long we disobey, You never
cease to give us another chance to get things right.
Thank you for Your grace and mercy as well as Your unending love.

Jealous God

Heavenly Father, nothing and no one should be placed
above You because You are a jealous God.
In Your Word You let us know jealous is not only
what You are, but it is also Your name.
Lord, You have made us who we are and given us everything we have.
You love us unconditionally, and You alone are our
protection. How could we put anything above You?

I think about the reactions of some people who are jealous.
Many times they get out of character and we seem to take
it in stride, thinking that somehow they are justified.
We think this because of the time they've put into a relationship,
the things they have given or what they have done.
How much more should You be justified when
You are the one who gave us life?
There is no "second" when it comes to You. You are second to none.
You should be first in everything and in every
way simply because of who You are.

We should not be surprised when the windows that You
opened in our lives begin to close because we placed You
second. We already know Your name is Jealous.
Nor should our blessed selves wonder what's going on when
we can no longer hear the answers to our prayers.
You have already told us who You are. Are
we expecting something different?
You are not a God who would lie nor can
You. If You say it then it is so.

So Father, just knowing that jealous is not only an attribute
with You, but it is also one of the ways You identify Yourself,
how can we lower You to any position less than You are?

No Sugar Added

Your Word is sharper than any two-edged sword.
It is given to us so we can live.
You said we are not to change it; not even the
dot of an "i" or the crossing of a "t".
So Father, there is no doubt in my mind
there should be no sugar added.

Your Word is just like medicine for the soul.
Even if receiving it makes us hurt a little,
just say ouch and keep it moving.
So often the preacher wants to make the Word
palatable, but that was never Your intent.
You don't want us breaking off the pieces of Word
we can tolerate or the parts that taste sweet.
You want us to eat the whole roll.

We are blessed to have Your Word to order our steps and direct our
paths. It wasn't available to those in the New or Old Testaments.
History is exactly what it is. We can't rewrite
it to make it what we want it to be.
If we had our way we would never go through anything which means
we would not allow You to bring us out of our trials and tribulations.

Your Word is our weapon to be used against the adversary.
We may not always understand why, but we
have to know that it's always right.
The Word will always work just the way You
designed it to with no sugar added.
Lord, we need to hide it in our hearts so we
can speak it out of our mouths.

Walking in Authority

Father, we need You to help us with our walk.
Sometimes it seems as if we are going in circles.
I don't know why we insist on majoring in minor things.
It seems we are doing what we don't do well, and
sometimes what we shouldn't do at all.
We need to come to the realization that You have given
us power and we should be walking in authority.

Lord You have already resurrected us from our dead
situations; we have a living hope in You.
I am convinced that some of us don't realize
what we have on the inside of us.
If we did we would take advantage of it.
Your Spirit resides in us enabling us to choose our lot in life.
We don't always have to resign ourselves to accept
what we see. We walk by faith and not by sight.
We have to speak some things out loud, bringing
them into existence, because words have power.

Father don't allow us to get comfortable in mediocrity when
greater is He that is in us than he that is in the world.
We need to be assured that walking in authority is what
You expect of us. It is what You have enabled us to do.
We need not fear the enemy nor should we give in to his tactics.
We should keep him under our feet for we
already have the victory in Christ Jesus.

My Time

It is often asked when will it be my time.
Surprisingly, the time we are seeking for is already within our grasp.
We just need to reach out and grab it.
"My time" seems to be evasive because we imagine it
to be a carbon copy of another individual's time.
However, what we are seeking for ourselves doesn't look like
someone else's because it is tailored specifically for us.

Many of us see in our mind's eye what we need to
do, but for some reason, tend not to do it.
We walk away from what we have been seeking for.
The question we need to ask ourselves is why.
Are we afraid to accept the responsibility that comes
along with the elusive "my time" or do we still need to
put in some work to make things fall into place.

Whatever the reason, it is really up to us to make it happen.
Father, You have given us everything we need to
be all that You have created us to be.
Don't let us stifle the "my time" that is trying to come
forth in order to accept mediocrity in any form.

Gifted Singleness

There is so much joy in marriage, and being
married is the best kind of life.
However, You have also given the gift of singleness to some who
won't get married and to others who must wait for marriage.
Lord, You are so wonderful. You know that we cannot handle
singleness alone, so Your gift of the Holy Spirit helps to keep us.
So often people neglect the beauty of being single because
they are so busy trying to become a couple.

Oftentimes, the opportunities that are present
are overlooked or seen as a hindrance.
Being able to flow with the Spirit and go
wherever He leads is a blessing.
Not having to be responsible to another actually
frees us to be used in different ways.
Freedom is God-given; singleness really does
allow us to serve without reservation.
As with many things, marriage comes with its own set of problems
that You are shielding us from at this point in our lives.
You are in control. You know what is best.

You may be still preparing the partner You want
us to have, or You may be preparing us for our
partner; either way it is coming, but not now.
Help us to grab hold of life the way You have given it to us.
We need to know that we are already
complete. We don't lack anything.
Teach us how to be content in our current state, then
let us be able to accept change when it comes.
When You created us You said it was not good for
man to be alone. Help us to wait on our soulmate
for life and not settle for a feel good night.

Hidden Delight

Your Word says we should delight ourselves in You.
Why is it we try to find delight in other places,
in other things or other people?
Are there times when we feel like we are missing out on something?
Do we reminisce about what used to be? Do we dare put ourselves
in situations that we believe we are strong enough to handle?
I pray not!

Lord, You are more than enough and yet we
find ourselves trying to add to You.
You are the I AM God. Whatever we need that's exactly what You are.
You sit high and look low, there is nothing hidden from Your view.
For this I am grateful because You have kept me from so
many things I didn't know were laying in wait for me.

Father You orchestrated my turn-arounds and my steps backward
and allowed me to bypass so much and for this I thank You.
Each of us comes from some place that we left behind when we
gave our lives to You, and yet, temptation comes and brags about
the hidden delight in the things we know we shouldn't partake in.

The enemy stays of his job to entice us with forbidden pleasures,
but it is Your Spirit that continues to lead and guide us.
Lord, I glorify Your name because You haven't isolated me
from the ways of the world, but You speak to me through
Your Word to help me maneuver through them.
Your Word says yield not to temptation. It
doesn't say temptation would not come.
All praises to You for always giving us a way out.

Closet Doors

Just like in the natural, closet doors are made to be opened and closed.
We open them to either put things in or take things out.
Sometimes we have items stored so far in the back that
we overlook them or maybe forget about them.
It is just like some things in us that we try to hide
deep in the recesses of our hearts and minds.
There are things we do not want to share with others.

We also have other things within us that we may be afraid
to expose, whether negative or actually positive.
Sometimes we purposely subdue great things You have placed within
us because we don't know how we will be accepted by others.
Help us realize that whatever You deposit
in us is to be poured out of us.
Whatever we have is not just for us, it is given for the body of Christ.

You have already told us to fear not.
I pray that we step out in faith to release all
that You have poured into us.
Father, my objective is to be completely
empty when You come for me.

New Creature

When we decided to follow You and were born
again, we became a new creature.
Your Word tells us that old things are past away,
behold, all things are become new.
There are, however, some who are still trying
to hold on to the old things.
We should be thinking differently, walking differently,
and our desires should be different.
The same old thing shouldn't hold our interest
any longer as we seek more of You.

Lord, I know that none of us are perfect and all of us still
have a sin nature, but I also know that the Holy Spirit is
trying to guide us and all we have to do is listen.
You have given us free will, but it is up to us
to choose to do the right thing.
Father, I pray that You help us to make the right choices
and not choose to go back to our old ways.
The only thing our old ways have to offer is spiritual death.

Heavenly Father, when we accepted You we received a new
life. We were introduced to love as we have never known it.
We received a zeal for all that is good, a newness in every
aspect of our being. We began to see things differently,
and had a desire to please You in everything we did.
We wanted to love others the same way You loved us.

I pray for us all. I pray that we go back to our first love…You!

Reveal It

So many of Your children are holding on
to things they need to let go of.
They are holding on to another life, another way of
doing things, a different set of rules, and so many
other things that are contrary to Your Word.
Lord, they didn't plan it and they don't like it.
They just can't seem to help themselves.
There is a stronghold on certain areas of
their lives and they can't get loose.

Lord, Your Word lets us know that some
things come by fasting and praying.
Your Word also says we should confess to one another. So many
people have a problem confessing due to the lack of confidentiality.
I pray they are led to someone trustworthy so they can reveal "it"
whatever their "it" is. Then powerful prayer can come forth.
Expose that thing. Bring it to light and let You handle the rest.

When we reveal it the enemy can no longer hold it over our heads.
We become free from that stronghold.
Thank You Father for giving Your children
a way out of fear and shame.
Don't hide it, reveal it.

A Difference

Father God, when we give ourselves to You a change
should occur causing a difference in us.
The song says I looked at my hands and they looked
new. I looked at my feet and they did too.
How true this song is. Everything about us becomes brand new.
So why is it that sometimes it is hard to tell
the Christian from the world?

Lord, I don't believe women have to wear skirts to their ankles, but
the hems of their skirts should not be near their waistlines either.
What is the point in that, what are women really saying?
We can look nice without showing all of our body parts.

Some of the things we used to do we no longer have a desire
for and I believe this happens in our dress as well.
If there are no changes in us are we really saved?
Father help us to step back and take long, hard look at ourselves.
We need to honestly assess what's going on with us.
We should reflect You.
Help us to see ourselves as You see us.

Narrow Way

Your Word says that straight is the gate and narrow is the
way which leadeth unto life, and few there be that find it.
This lets us know that following You will not be an easy task, but
if we want eternal life with You we must take the narrow way.
The narrow way does not allow for willful sin. Going
this way we cannot give in to our emotions.
In other words we can't do what we want to do or what feels
good. You said we should pick up our cross and follow You.

Lord, You don't expect us to do the impossible,
although it sounds like we can't do it.
The truth is, we can't do it without You.
You promised You would never leave us or forsake us, so You are
always there to do what we can't do. You said to cast our cares on You.
You are God who makes a way out of no way.

Father I want to walk that narrow way so that
I can see You one day face to face.
This way is not easy, and You didn't say it would be.
I go through storms and sometimes I find myself
in valleys, but then there are those mountaintop
experiences that make everything else worth it.
I seem to forget the hard time, but it is those times
that prepare me to get to the mountaintop.
The narrow way may be rough, but it is worth it.

Justified Suicide

When is suicide alright? How can we justify it? It
is never alright and there is no justification.
You are the giver of life and You decide when life ends.
Yet, we do things that we know will shorten our lives
and then we try to justify our right to do it.
I am speaking about our physical lives, but we
do the same things in our spiritual lives.

We refuse to release what You have placed in us, hoping to
"kill" it because we don't want to do it, don't want to speak
it, or don't want to go where You're trying to send us.
We withhold without realizing we are attempting to
commit suicide to something You said was good.
Maybe we cannot understand, maybe we are afraid or
maybe we think we will be unfairly judged by others.
Whatever our reason, there is no justified suicide.
We must yield to Your will and Your ways.

Although You have given us emotions, we are not to be led by them.
We are to follow the Spirit as He leads us.
Lord, help us to understand our actions, help us to see the affects of
our inactivity; show us the unnecessary burden we place on ourselves.
Remind us that we were created for Your use.
You are Lord of Lords and King of Kings. We
should bow down to Your majesty.

Loud Silence

It is such a blessing to be teachable; otherwise, I would
never have known that silence has a voice.
The voice is extremely loud, and most times it
speaks when we're trying not to be noticed.
I am grateful for the lessons You've given me.
I've learned there are times when I must speak up and speak out.
Remaining quiet when I don't agree says I'm with you
whether you're wrong or right; and not speaking up
for what I know to be right, makes me a sellout.
Loud silence is talking all the time, especially when
a response or rebuke should be forthcoming.

Lord, what about those who are unable to speak up for themselves?
It is my opportunity to speak on their behalf.
Somebody has to be concerned and it can start with me.
I don't need to wait for someone else to say that's
not right or this is not God's way.
I can't concern myself with what people think, I must
be Your mouthpiece and speak when You lead me.

Sometimes I need to be silent, and during the times
my silence isn't talking, it is acting appropriately;
I just need to know when those times are.
I should never be the one who is trying to go along to get along.
It should not be in my character to imitate someone
else; I must be true to who You created me to be.
We're like snowflakes, no two are alike.

Sometimes I have to speak things into existence. Other times I may need to encourage. Then there are the times I have to let the enemy know that he's a defeated foe. Your desire is that I boldly speak the Word.
Thank You for teaching me how to handle the words You've placed in me.

Flocked Up

Lord, very often Your people seem to stay amongst themselves.
They are like birds, flocked up with their own kind.
Our job is to go beyond the church walls to
compel the unbeliever to come to You.
We should be walking epistles, in other words, billboards, for Christ.

When we read our Bibles we learn that Jesus
was in the midst of the people.
His first miracle was at a wedding, not at the synagogue.
He was at the tax collector's house, in a boat,
with the multitude, not always at church.

We should also be where the people are.
We are sheep and sheep beget sheep.
Therefore, we should bring others to the
church so they may learn of You.
Sometimes we only demonstrate our life in You on Sundays.

We need to be transparent 24/7. People should
be able to look through us and see You.
Help us to be mindful that You work through people.
You need to use our hands, our mouths,
and our feet for Your purposes.

We need to step out of our comfort zone and into the battle field.
The enemy is a defeated foe because You have already won the battle.
Father, I am thanking You in advance for reminding us that we don't
do anything in our own strength, it is You who stands tall within us.

Soul Eclipse

A solar eclipse occurs when the moon passes between the
earth and the sun, blocking the light of the sun and a
shadow of the moon is cast on the earth's surface.
Lord, when we allow anything to get between You
and us this is what I call a soul eclipse.
When we get so involved in things and people that we can no
longer keep You in our view, it is time for some soul searching.
We have lost our first love and have replaced
You with the things of this world.
Father help us to know that the things we can see won't
last. We need to keep our focus on what is eternal.

I am so grateful that You are God of another chance.
It doesn't matter how far we have fallen; we
can always repent and return to You.
Lord, open our spiritual eyes so that we are not
deceived by what looks good to us.
Open our spiritual ears so that sweet words don't sway
us back to the places we have traveled from.
Help us to step up so that we no longer live
beneath the place where You put us.
When we step up, let us then stand up on
the Rock who is Jesus Christ.
Remind us that when You are our main
focus we will rise up victorious.

Cover Up

I wonder if our religious activity is just a cover up for the real us.
Fraud is running rampant. People go to church, work
in the church, even appear churchy; but their lives
outside of the church paint another picture.
Busyness is a substitute for relationship.
People want to give others the appearance that they
are holy, when in fact, they are hollow.
They don't have anything on the inside that
can reflect You on the outside.

Oftentimes, people will volunteer to work on several
committees and ministries, while also singing on the choir
and bring a Word from the pulpit; but they are not real.
The word that best describes them is hypocrite.
Lord, they need to know that although You're longsuffering,
at some point You will pull the cover off.

You gave Your Son for the sins of the world.
He died that we might have the right to the Tree of Life.
When we accept Him, He covers us in His blood.
Why would we then choose to cover up in anything else?

Lord, we cannot fool You. You are the creator and we
are the creation. Our pretense only fools us.

Dream Deferred

Lord, it's amazing how we dream and make
plans for a future that You control.
I realize that there is no harm in having a vision,
because without a vision we perish.
However, the issue is, does our vision line up with Your will.
Father, help me to always be mindful to stay in
prayer concerning Your will for my life.

Help me to know that although I may have
aspirations and desires, the timing is Yours.
You may need to complete a work in me before I can proceed.
There may be some things that I am not yet ready to handle.
How about the experiences that I must have in
order to do or be what You desire for me?

What a blessing to know that sometimes my dream must be deferred
so that You can provide for me what I could never think or see.
Your thoughts are far beyond my thoughts;
and You desire the very best for me.
That's what a loving father does; gives the very best He has.

I may not always expect what You bring my
way, but I know it's what I need.
I may want You to move quicker, but I know You're always on time.
I don't always understand Your ways, but You told
me not to lean to my own understanding.
Hallelujah! My eyes have been opened to see that my dream
is deferred because you are perfecting it just for me.

Purposeful Living

I heard the preacher say "in purpose on purpose"
and that struck a chord within me.
He is absolutely right. You put purpose within
each of us and we should be walking in it.
We should be prayerful and conscience about living
in our individual purposes on purpose.

It is not necessarily about what we desire for ourselves,
but it is about the purpose we were created to fulfill.
Your Word lets us know that our destiny was
predetermined before we were born.
You gave us our gifts and talents, even our unquenchable desires.
When it seemed like we wouldn't be satisfied until we
met some specific goal in life, that was You leading and
guiding us into the purpose You had placed in us.

Lord, You said not to lean to my own understanding, but to
acknowledge You in all my ways and You would direct my path.
Your Word is true and I am determined to allow
You to fulfill Your purpose within me.

Sacred Togetherness

When love comes, we often say the person has completed us.
That is not really true since we were already complete.
When the love of our lives is manifested, they tend to introduce
us to parts of ourselves that only they are able to reveal to us.
Just imagine having the love of another along
with Your love; what a blessed life that is.
Loving You while loving and being loved by the physical
other that You intended us to have is awesome.

We were created to be intertwined with another.
After all, You created male and female together and
then You pulled the woman out of the male so she
could be with him rather than within him.
So often we take our mates for granted, overlooking
the magnificent sacredness of our togetherness.
Help us to cherish our marriages. Each day
we share is a blessing from You.

You intended that marriage be between a man and woman.
No opposition, law decree, ordinance or
any other thing can change that.
Even if people don't agree with it, it is still true.
Marriage, in its true form, defined by Your Word, is a blessing.
Help us to honor it and each other.

Surrender All

Lord, there have been times when I didn't
know where to turn or what to do.
I couldn't see beyond my right now.
You spoke to my heart and said that I should surrender all.
Thank You for letting me know what to do
when I didn't know what to do.

You don't want certain parts and pieces of my life, You desire all of it.
It is not up to me to offer some aspects of my life and not others.
You said surrender all.
All is a three letter word, but it includes everything; nothing left out.
I have been set apart for your use; that includes
all of me. My complete self is yours.

Lord, You can use my mouth to speak words of life to Your people.
You can use my hands to serve and my feet to go where You direct.
You can use the money You have given me
for building up Your kingdom.
You can use my eyes to see the need in situations and
people that others may not want to get involved with.
You can use my ears to hear what others are really saying
when their words are saying something else.
Father, I pray that You have Your way with me as I surrender all.

Open Spaces

As I look out over the land I see great open
spaces; an expanse of Your creation.
I think about Your people and pray there
are no open spaces within us.
I pray that we have saturated ourselves with Your Spirit.

I pray that every crevice and fold is filled, so
that there is no room for evil to dwell.
I pray that doubt is dissipated and only
faith in You remains within us.
Heavenly Father, I pray that the Holy Spirit occupies
the temple that is within Your people.

Grateful Praise

I am grateful for release from stagnation while going
nowhere fast by allowing myself to stand still.
That is not what You want for me.
Your Word declares that I should bear fruit; that my
mind should be renewed and I should grow in grace.
I am grateful for release from feelings of inadequacies
because my accomplishments are brushed to the side.

Father, It is not about me, it is all about You.
All that I do and say is for Your glory, not
for any recognition on my part.
I must always remember that I can do nothing without You.
I am grateful to no longer march to the beat of society's
drum, but I am able to dance to the song You have put
in my heart for the victory that is already won.

Clinging Vine

There are some people who cling to others because
at some point they were abandoned.
These people don't know how to let go.
They have problems releasing because they think
they may lose what they are clinging to.

We tend to hold on for dear life when we believe our lives are
predicated on someone or something, other than You.
Help us to see that being abandoned wouldn't pertain
to us if we put our trust in You and not in people.
You said You would never leave us or forsake us, so
we don't have to be clinging vines holding on to a
false sense of security. We are secure in You.

Father, I thank You for being constant in my life. You have
always been there; even when it seemed like I was alone.
You are omnipresent; everywhere at the same time.

Interior Design

Father, thank You for making changes in me.
You didn't look at my exterior, but You looked on the inside.
Lord, You saw the necessity for a complete renovation within me.
You didn't just spruce me up, but You gave
me a brand new interior design.

The work You did on the inside of me showed up on the outside.
Because my mind was made new, I thought
differently about how I appeared to the world.
I didn't want my appearance to say things
about me that did not apply.

I no longer hold my head down because
You are the lifter up of my head.
My frown has been turned upside down
because You gave me unspeakable joy.
No longer do I put off until tomorrow what I can
do today because I must redeem the time.

Lord, I am grateful for the transformation within me.
You have knocked down the emotional walls that I erected.
Now I am no longer led by my emotions, but
by the Word coming from You.

When I look in my spiritual mirror everything may not always
appear as it should, but I thank You God, that I can always
call on the interior designer to make the necessary changes.

Stinking Thinking

You said my mind should be like Yours; well,
sometimes my mind is in left field.
My mind seems to do its own thing and takes off running.
What would I do without Your Word?
It lets me know that I should have control over my thoughts, that
I can bring them into captivity in order to be obedient to You.

Father, my stinking thinking tries to take over; yet,
Your word tells me what to think about.
It says think on things that are true, honest,
just, pure, lovely and of a good report.
You didn't say just do it, You tell me how.

I can do all things through Christ, even control my mind.
Lord, my soul rejoices in the abundance of Your love
Thank You for being in me what I cannot be for myself.

Wounded Soldiers

There have been times when I have been wounded in the battle.
Like me, countless wounded soldiers can
be found in the body of Christ.
All of the wounds have not been inflicted
by the enemy, but by the church.
It is called friendly fire, but there's nothing friendly about it.
Our armor doesn't include guns and yet too often we are shot down.

Our battle is not against people, but against
principalities; it's not natural but spiritual.
We put on truth, righteousness, the gospel of peace,
the shield of faith, helmet of salvation and the sword
of the spirit, which is the Word of God.
We are not trying to destroy our brothers and sisters.
Our intent is to uplift and encourage one another,
since we all must stand against the devil.

Lord, show us ourselves, let us see our actions for what they really are.
Please don't allow us to continue to hurt each
other and call it constructive criticism.
Teach us that our opinions belong to us and
don't have to be given to others.
Since they are ours let us keep them, unless someone asks for them.

Father, show us that words can be like bullets,
damaging to the core. Some words are even fatal.

Down Low

Heavenly Father, Your Word says if I am ashamed
of You now, You will be ashamed of me later.
I know that Your Word is true, so I am trying
to take heed to all that You say.
Lord why do some people try to serve You on the down low?
We must always lift You up. Then You will lift others to Yourself.

We cannot treat You as if You are insignificant when
You are King of kings and Lord of lords.
You are the all-knowing God and You are present in every place.
Nothing is hidden from You. You see how we pretend before others.
We try to fit in when, in fact, we should stand out.

Our desire to be accepted by the world is
contrary to all that we should be about.
We should proclaim Your name from the rooftops.
Our walk should be upright. We should not be ducking and hiding.
You said we should be hot or cold. We cannot
straddle the fence and expect Your blessings.
Lord, You are holy and we should reverence You.
Help us to recognize the damage that we bring to ourselves.

Whatever we bow down to becomes our God.
Father, help us not to worship Your creation. You alone are the one
who makes the wind blow. You make the sun shine and the rain fall.
We need to be mindful that You are a jealous God.

My desire is to serve You with all that is in me.
You are great and greatly to be praised.
I don't want to be where You are not welcome
because I can't do anything without you.
I shall always glorify You because all that I have seen
teaches me to trust You for all that I have not seen.

Unbelieving Believer

Lord, when the words unbelieving and believer are
put together it makes absolutely no sense at all.
How can we call ourselves believers and remain unbelieving?
As strange as it sounds, it happens everyday.

I have listened to many who complain about their situation,
are worried about their finances, and think the worse about
their circumstances; and yet they call themselves believers.
I wonder in who or what do they believe.

Your Word tells us that You will supply our needs.
It also says if we first seek Your kingdom and Your
Righteousness, all these things will be added.
Lord, You will provide food, shelter and clothing. These
are basic needs that You know are necessary.

Missed Opportunity

At times I didn't go when You sent me.
Then there were the occasions I didn't do things Your way.
In each instance, I was out of Your will because
I did what I thought was best.
You do things in Your own time and Your timing is perfect.
Your ways are not our ways, neither are Your thoughts our thoughts.
You are the Almighty who knows what is best.

Father, my missed opportunity to minister to someone
before they transitioned was my own fault.
You sent me at the right time, but I was busy
with another matter, and I went later.
My later was too late.

When I struggled with the way to solve a particular
problem; You responded with the answer, but because I
couldn't see things Your way, I chose another option.
Had I listened to You my path would have been so much easier.
Lord, a missed opportunity that is recognized for what it
is helps us to see our mistakes and learn from them.
We don't know everything and we need to
depend on You for all things.

Thank You for giving us free will. You don't force
things on us; instead, You let us choose.
Our choices aren't always right, but the one
thing that is constant is You.
We don't always do the right thing, but You still love us,
You still remain with us and You lovingly correct us.
Father, Your will is always my right choice.

Still Waters

It is said that still waters run deep and this can describe many people.
We may not see too much on the outside, but
on the inside there is a lot going on.
Shallow water and shallow people have a lot in common.
The shallower the water the more turbulence is visible.
Shallow people are always talking about themselves or other
people and they always have some type of drama going on.

People who appear calm and collected are like deep, still waters,
where the turbulence is deep down and not seen on the surface.
They are deep thinkers and are not outwardly
disturbed by external circumstances.
Father, You told us to let our words be few.
You said we should meditate day and night.

If we are obedient to Your Word, we won't have time
to talk about things that are not important.
Lord, please guard the gates of our mouths.
Help us to think before we speak.
Let our words edify, encourage and build up.

Praise Report

Every day that You keep waking me up is reason to give You praise.
I always have a praise report, because I
cannot take anything for granted.
I know I can't do anything without You, so whenever
I get something done that is a praise.
When I see how You bought me out of yesterday when
I thought I couldn't make it; that is a praise.

Let me take a moment to give You glory for saving my soul.
My salvation is priceless.
My relationship with You is a praise.

Father, Your love for me is a praise report!

Politically Correct

Father, why are Christians afraid to stand on Biblical truths?
You need bold, not coward, soldiers in Your army.
We must speak the words that You have spoken.
Changing them to fit a situation for a few people won't work.
You have already told us if we even change the crossing of
a "t" or the dotting of an "i" there are consequences.

Too often, we compromise and label it as being politically correct.
What do politics have to do with anything?
Politics don't supersede Your Word.
We are the peculiar ones. We should be speaking out against those
things You speak against; and yet, we are actually in agreement.

We seem to blend in with the world, because
it is hard to see a difference.
Our presence in the world should be like a neon sign….noticeable.
Our presence should make a difference.
Lord help us to get back to where we used to be.
Remind us that this is not our home, we are just passing through.

Stretch Out

I am so blessed not to have to rely on myself to make
sense out of things I have no control over.
Lord, I can stretch out on You.
Everything that happens in life is because You allow it.
Sometimes I am so excited that I can hardly contain myself.
Other times, I try to understand what I need
to learn from my circumstance.
Then there are the times when it seems as if my
very soul has been ripped from within me.
Whatever happens I can stretch out on You.

I don't always have a feel good experience.
My feelings don't really matter. What is most
important is that I can always come to You.
When I stretch out, I am giving everything I feel to You.
Then I am able to bring my emotions to a
place where they cannot control me.
I can give You praise even when I want to pull away in despair.
I can give You glory when I would rather drown in my tears.
Father, I can lift You up even while I am still down.

Major Purpose

We must walk in purpose on purpose.
We cannot give space to self-doubt and fear.
You have placed major purpose within each of us.
You have poured into us what will bring glory to You.

Father, there are times when we want to choose our way.
Your Word says that You are the way, truth and life.
None of us were created to do our own thing.
We were created to fulfill the purposes that serve Your will.
Help us to realize that we are the creation and You are the creator.

True awakening comes when we realize just who we are;
when we recognize exactly what we should do.

True Beauty

We make so many decisions based on outward appearances.
Sometimes we even choose whether to speak or not to
speak to a person solely based on how they look.

Lord, I am thankful that is not how You do things.
You look at our hearts. You see the true beauty that
radiates from the inside out. When true beauty is
evident, it cannot help but show up on the outside.

True beauty cannot be seen with the eye; it is an attribute that shows
itself through our actions. It demonstrates the fruit of the spirit.
People may not always recognize it by name, but they certainly feel it.

As we strive to be more like You our true beauty will become
evident to everyone we come in contact with. Please help me
to work on my shortcomings so that my true beauty comes
forth. In this way people will really see You through me.

In Position

Lord, help me to be in position to receive all that You have for me. If I am not where I should be, then I miss out. Father, I don't want to be absent from the blessing You have designed for me.

When You direct my path and order my steps, You are setting me up to receive. However, if I don't follow Your direction I end up blocking my own blessing.

Sometimes we think we have all the answers and decide to do things our own way, but Your ways are not our ways, neither are Your thought our thoughts. So, we end up standing back and looking at what could have been.

Father, I know what is for me is for me, but I also know You do things in Your time; not mine. If I veer off from Your schedule I could miss out or have to wait longer. So Lord, help me to position myself to be in Your will.

I want my yes to be heard because I am in sync with you; let me be where I am supposed to be.

As You lead, I will follow.

Chosen Vessel

Lord, I didn't choose You. You chose me. I am Your chosen vessel to work through. This is not something I take for granted, nor is it anything I deserve. It is just a fact.

You work through people and we have to be susceptible to You. My prayer is that You use me as You see fit; I am yielded to You.

Although You have given me free will, I desire that Your will be my will. Just like a bond servant, I want to serve You with all that is in me.

As a chosen vessel, I have to live for You. I cannot allow the world to use me as a receptacle for its deposits of filth and deceit. I can't absorb what the world throws my way. My mind must be focused on You.

It is not about me, it is all about You. I need to be conformed to Your likeness.
Have Your way with me Lord. Use all that You have placed in me so that You will be glorified.

Father, when You get ready to take me to Yourself, let me be an empty vessel.

Recycled Life

Lord, I know who I am in You; however, I remember
when I was thrown away like trash by the world.
I can flash back to a time when I was being used, not for my own
benefit, but so that others would see themselves as better than me.
I can recall being stepped on and kicked to the side
so that somebody else could rise to the top.
I don't mind helping others succeed, but I don't want
to be bruised and battered in the process.
Lord, I know that is not what You desire either.

Father, in spite of what has happened to me You came to my rescue.
You picked me up and used what had been discarded.
You recycled a life that was thought to be good for nothing.
My life was completely turned around.
You demonstrated that we can't put our trust in
what we see, but in what we can't see.

Lord, You are Spirit and yet You moved on my behalf.
I can't see You, but I know that You are.
I have been recycled and I am trying with all
that is in me to bring You glory.
My life is Your life; it no longer belongs to me.
When I was in control, I messed things up,
now I yield myself to Your will.
Thank You for revealing Your plans for my life.
Thank You for giving me the determination to
give back to You all that is within me.

Denied Destiny

Lord, You have our future in Your hands. You created
us and You placed our destiny inside of us.
Help us to stop denying our rightful place within the earth.
Too often we decide what we will and will not do; where we
will and will not go and what we will and will not say.
However, your Word tells us what to do, where to
go and what to say and we should obey.

Somehow we begin to think that our desires
supersede Your will for our lives.
We need to understand that it is not about us, but it is all about You.
You are God, the creator, and we are your creation.
At no time does the creation tell the Creator
how things are supposed to operate.

Father, we have allowed ourselves to get beyond ourselves
to the point that we think we're in charge.
Your Word lets me know that every knee will bow and every
tongue will confess. It is time that we get on our knees to repent.
It seems that repentance isn't practiced much because
most of the time people don't think they're wrong.

People have used the Scripture to make it say what they
want it to say, not what You intend it to say to us.
This has caused a denied destiny to many. You didn't deny it,
we denied ourselves simply because we didn't do our part.
You are a promise keeper, and we need to walk in faith and
obedience to Your Word to see the manifestation of Your promises.

Unmet Expectations

We intend to meet goals and deadlines we set for ourselves.
However, there are circumstances that may
keep us from our expected end.
I've named it unmet expectations.
Father, we rarely think we're at fault, but tend to play the blame game.
Our situations changed, money was funny
or someone didn't do their part.

Help us to see there are times when adjustments
need to be made; times when goals need to be
modified or deadlines need to be extended.
We shouldn't fall into the trap of thinking that
mistakes in judgment are total failures.
Maybe You never intended the same outcome we expected.
Did we ever consult You?

Lord, whatever You do, You do it well.
You will take what was meant for evil and use it for our good.
We should always put You first in our plans
because our plans should also be Your will.
We must remember that He who hath begun a good
work in us will perform it until Jesus Christ.

Stop Worrying

Lord, I wonder if we have ever thought about Your
promises to us. You promised to supply our needs.
So why do we continue to worry about the things of this world?
We need to stop worrying, because all worry
does is show our lack of faith in You.
If we worry, there's no need to pray and if we believe
when we pray, there's no need to worry.

Our witness doesn't amount to much when we are
always worrying about one thing or the other.
Even if we're not talking about it, somehow
worry shows up in our countenance.
People shouldn't know that we are concerned about
anything; just that our trust is in You.
Father, Your word says be anxious for nothing,
and we should take you at Your word.

Help us to concentrate more on what we have
and not on what we don't have.
Too often, we overlook the many ways we have been
blessed because we're busy trying to get more.
We need to stop and smell the roses while
we're still amongst the living.
Worry shortens our life span, it causes stress and stress kills.
We need to stop worrying and trust You.

Driven Praise

There is nothing that will keep me from giving You praise.
When I think about Your goodness my soul cries out.
You sent Your son to die for my sins and not
for me only, but for the whole world.
How could I not give You all the glory? I have a driven
praise, all I have to do is think and praise comes forth.
Lord, You are a wonder in my soul.

Your description defies words since You are beyond
anything my mind can comprehend.
If I tried to say it I would put You in a box, thereby constricting
You to what I know and You're so much more than that.
I could never do justice by applauding You with my mouth,
but the spirit within me leaps at the mention of Your name.

Lord, You are everything to me. Without You there is nothing
The fact that I get to worship You blows my
mind because this is why I was created.
My "thank you" seems meager; I really desire to offer my
obedience to Your will and Your way in all things.
I am Your yielded vessel Lord. Have Your own way.

Leftovers Revisited

Lord, most of the time we think negatively about
leftovers. They are what remains from some other time;
not something we intentionally planned for today.
When we think of leftover food, some things taste
better a day or two after they have been prepared. This
allows time for the spices to blend together.
Think about pasta.
Then, there are leftover pains that may still be felt after
a severe illness or accident; little uncomfortable twinges
that remind us of what we've been through.

Well Father, I wonder is it always necessary to
feel pain associated with another time, or can we
remember there was pain and just move pass it?
Why do we constantly talk about it, thereby keeping it alive and well?
There is no reason to dwell on pain. We should feel free to let it go.
Everything happens for a reason. When we have
gleaned from our painful experiences we can let
that pain go. Life is ongoing, not stagnant.

Are we actually seeking pity from others? Do we
want people to feel sorry for us? Or, is pain the only
way we can draw attention to ourselves?
It is one thing to deal with painful situations then
testify about it in order to help someone else.
It's something else when we constantly relive
it, and can't seem to move pass it.
Lord help us to look to You and not stay stuck in a hurtful place.

118

Holding Pattern

Father, sometimes You tell us to halt. You want us to remain
still, while You hold us. That's what a holding pattern is.

Just like airplanes, waiting for permission to land.
Sometimes You need for us to stop trying to move to
another place in our own strength and just allow You
to hold us and take complete control of our lives.

You know the beginning, as well as, the end of a situation; and
You will allow all things to come to fruition in Your time.

Before we can move from one level to another, we must go
through a process. If we move too soon failure might be in
our future and if we don't move soon enough, we could miss
opportunities. If we wait on You everything comes together.

Expanded Borders

Heavenly Father, it is a blessing to realize that we don't just go to church, but that we are the church.

So often we get caught up in the brick and mortar instead of souls.

When we realize that we are the church we will understand that we need expanded borders. We must extend beyond ourselves to reach those who don't know You.

Lord, give me a burden for lost souls. Show me how to step outside of myself and into the life of someone You have prepared to received You.

Family Matters

There are times when we come together as a family, leaving out close
friends and acquaintances because we need to discuss family matters.
But, there should also be a time when we recognize how
important these people truly are because family matters.
As I look around I see that the family is coming apart at the seam.
Father, You intended the family to consist of a man,
who is father; a woman, who is mother and children,
but in many instances it's totally different.

It seems that the enemy began to dismantle family a while
ago. He started with the head of the family, the father.
I don't know what happened, but many of them were no longer
part of the family unit. Not all fathers fall in this category, but
those who do have made a huge difference in the family structure.
The enemy is on his job, he starts with the strong man
just as he does when he tries to destroy a church.
We have to recognize his tactics and stop falling for his gimmicks.

Father help us to see that we need strong families. Whatever
the enemy tries to tear down is reason for us to build up.
Don't allow us to get caught up in the hype. The real
deal is that men and women produce children and we
can't change Your order of how things should be.
When we attempt to do that we take ourselves into the unfamiliar.
You are the only one who knows what that ending looks like.
Lord bring us back to Your way

Stay Connected

I never want to be apart from You and I am thankful that can't
happen because You said You would never leave me or forsake me.
Lord, I'm so grateful for salvation because
I couldn't make it otherwise.
Sure, I haven't always been saved and I thought I was
doing fine when I wasn't, but when I came into the
knowledge of You my whole world changed.
My mind was renewed so I started thinking differently.

Father, I have to always stay connected to
You because You are my lifeline.
As I read Your Word, I hear You speaking to me. I know that the
words in the Bible are more than words on paper. They are alive!
The Words order my steps and direct my path.
The Bible is able to speak to any situation I may be going through.
There is absolutely nothing missing that pertains to life.

I believe we sometimes talk too much with people
who we think have all the answers.
If only we would spend more time with You we would
find that You alone are more than enough.
Lord thank You for direction and encouragement.
Thank you for helping me to stay connected.

Nevertheless Praise

We are always praising You and lifting You
up when things are going well.
However, our voices cease to express favor
when things don't go our way.
Your Word says that You inhabit the praises of Your people.
This statement alone should encourage us to give you praise always.
Our praise should not be predicated upon our situations.

Somewhere within us we should have a nevertheless praise
on standby, just waiting for the opportunity to show up.
It is during the rough times that we need to pick up the pace.
We know You can make a way out of no way; we know You are
more than enough and we know You can do anything but fail.
So, we need to praise our way through.

Too often Christians are holding their heads down
when they should be giving You glory.
Our joy should always be on display because
You are living on the inside of us.
You are great and greatly to be praised.
So, whenever trials or tribulation come our way we should insert
our nevertheless praise in the midst of it and watch You work.

Holy Confidence

It is a blessing when we know it is going to
be even though we can't see it yet.
I call this holy confidence.

We don't get impatient, because we know
You will do things in Your time.
Lord, we don't try to rush You along or do things in our
strength; we just trust You to make it happen.

Father, You are faithful. Your promises are yea and
amen. If You said it, then it shall be so.

We don't have to wonder about it. We can just walk
in holy confidence knowing that it is as good as done.
You do everything perfectly and right on time.

Your ways are not our ways and Your thoughts are not our
thoughts. You are beyond what we know and pass figuring out.

However, You have no problem revealing more and more of
Yourself to us as we continue to yield ourselves to You.

No matter what our struggles may be, You always come to our rescue.
You never leave us stranded in any situation and
You always love us through adversity.

Lord, You are as concerned about our issues as we are. It is
Your pleasure to be available to us at all times and Father,
it is my pleasure to put all things in Your hands.

Unequally Yoked

Lord, so many marriages are on the outs. It
seems there are problems in every area.
Your Word tells us that we should not be unequally
yoked and I believe therein lies the problem.
People want to be married but they don't take
the time to marry the right person.
They choose not to really get to know their partners.
Many times they see the warning signs, but they ignore them because
they don't want anything to interfere with their wedding day.

Why do they decide to suffer rather than
flourish in a lifelong relationship?
You created marriage and You said the two would become one.
Father, light and darkness don't have anything in
common, so how can the marriage work?
You never intended that Mrs. become a status symbol,
but that man would have his partner for life.

Some people consider marriage as safe sex. My question to them is
what happens if one partner can no longer perform due to sickness or
an accident. What else do they have to keep the home fires burning?
Father, we seem to overlook everything that is important in favor
of those things that might make us happy or make us feel good.
We must remember that happiness is not joy. It won't last forever
and there will be times when we won't feel good either.

Lord, You patterned Your love for the church after
marriage. So we must understand that it is so
much more than a beautiful wedding day.

Marriage is two lives entwined in love. Two lives who forsake all others and love each other in spite of every obstacle they may face. It is love the way You love us. It suffers long and is kind, doesn't find fault, doesn't envy, doesn't parade itself, isn't puffed up, doesn't behave rudely, doesn't seek its own, is not provoked, thinks no evil, does not rejoice in iniquity but rejoices in the truth; bears all things, believes all things, hopes all things, endures all things.

Love never fails.

Not Yet

If not yet then when. Father, we hear it all the time. People constantly say not yet, I'm not ready, I'm too young, I have to get myself together first or I have time, just not yet.

Lord, we don't know the day or the hour when You will come for Your people. One thing is sure, You are coming and on that day it will be too late to get ready.

When I hear "not yet," my heart breaks because it seems there is no way to convince them that today is the day of salvation. There is nothing they can do to get ready. All they can do is accept the gift of salvation and allow You to do the rest.

Not yet is a trick of the enemy. He attempts to give a false sense of security, making people think that somehow they have control over Your timing.

Accidents happen all the time and we don't have an opportunity to accept You or to repent. That is why it behooves us to BE ready at all times.

Lord, I pray for those who don't know You in the pardon of their sins. I pray they will come while they still have time.

Desert Storm

When we think of Desert Storm, we recall a military conflict. This
same terminology can be applied to a life lived without You.
A desert is dry, barren and usually uninhabited,
that's how living without You would be.
I imagine a storm forming in such a place. Where could I
run, or who could I run to? Father, I can only see a bleak
picture of something I wouldn't want any part of.

I am so thankful for salvation and I don't take it for granted.
I can remember when joy was not a part of my
life and I'm not trying to revisit the past.
Storms come into my life now, but I am well
prepared to weather these storms.
I know You will help me go through them.
Even though I can't see You, I know that You are always with me.
I am never alone.

Wearing Camouflage

Father, as I look at my surroundings I see people wearing camouflage.
I am not in the military, but camouflage is all around me.
It seems to show up in the most unexpected
places…churches for example.

So many people are sitting in churches with broad smiles
on their faces, but they are wearing camouflage.
Camouflage is worn to make you blend in with your surroundings.
I am grateful that You let me see this. You give us
discernment so the enemy can't fool us.

The smiles are fake and the words that come
from their mouths are insincere.
Their actions give them away every time.
They are not real, acting one way around one group of
people and completely different around another group.
No love is shown, where is it? You can't be Christ-like without love.

I thought charity began at home so how can
family members be mistreated?
Lord, You gave us the ministry of reconciliation.
I guess it was overlooked and not applied.
Father, help us to put on Jesus and take the camouflage off.

Bitter Herbs

Life will have good times and bad times.
Everyday won't be filled with happiness and laughter.
Sometimes we will go through things that
seem to suck the life out of us.
But these are the storms that come to make us strong.

Following the original Passover, when the Death Angel
passed the Israelites by; they left Egypt in a hurry.
Before departing they ate unleavened bread and bitter herbs.
Unleavened bread because they couldn't wait for the bread to rise.
Bitter herbs to be a reminder of their bitter
experiences while in bondage.

You told them they should always celebrate
Passover by eating these same things.
Lord we should also remember where You have bought us from.

You had to reach way down to get some of us.
We didn't all come from the same place, but
we came from places riddled with sin.
It is only because of Your grace and mercy
that we are able to testify today.

I want to celebrate where You have bought me from
by symbolically eating my bitter herbs.
Show me how to commemorate my salvation.
I walked away from many things that I never want to return to.
I trust You to show me how to celebrate.

Dry Places

Heavenly Father, there are times when we
experience dry places in our walk with You.
Since You operate in seasons, it stands to reason we do
also. There will be times when we may not function
as we usually do; because trouble is all around.
There will be times when we can't pray for ourselves and
have to rely on others to intercede on our behalf.
Maybe there will be times when it just seems
as if our relationship is out of rhythm.

These are the dry places that we sometimes travel
through. We could call them our winter seasons.
We don't stay there, we simply work through them.
The one thing we have to stay cognizant of is that we
must not die spiritually while in dry places.
We can't allow the enemy to get the upper hand. We
must always remember that he is already defeated.

Sometimes we look at our problems instead of looking at our God.
Lord, You are the problem solver. There is
nothing that can stand in Your way.
You are an impossibility specialist. There is nothing You can't do.

Dry places are hurdles we have to jump over.
Father, I thank You for letting me recognize
dry places for what they are.
They are seasons I have to have enough faith to go through.
Since I live by faith, not by sight; no matter what
it looks like, I am well able to overcome.

Strange Fruit

Lord, You said we would be known by the fruit we bear.
You were speaking about the fruit of the Spirit: love, joy, peace,
longsuffering, gentleness, goodness, faith, meekness and temperance.
How is it that we sometimes project strange
fruit and call ourselves Christians?

We might be advertising our fruit of jealousy, envy or
backbiting, while professing our Christlikeness.
We are really pulling You down and not lifting You up.

Our actions tell the real story. Lord, let us be mindful
of the fact that people are watching us.
We should emulate You and not give in to what our flesh wants to do.
We are Your ambassadors, walking in the earth representing You.

Father, help us to turn away from all that is not like You.
Open our eyes to who You really are.
You are our Holy God, not to be played with, but to be reverenced.
I bow down to Your majesty and pray that I don't just
have a form of Godliness, but that God dwells in me.

Thank You

Father, You are more than enough. Words can't adequately explain what that actually means to me.

All I know for sure is that You are the fulfillment of the desires I haven't wanted yet.

You are the completion of those things that haven't yet begun.

You are beyond what I can express and You surpass what my imagination can envision.

Lord, You are above all and the Creator of everything and yet, You are always with me.

You speak to my heart.

You order my steps.

You love me.

Thank You!

New Sighted

It is such a blessing to hear the preached Word. It is then, that You are
able to open my eyes and my mind to what I could not see before.
You gave us the preacher to make things clear to us and I am grateful.
I now know that I don't always have to desire something
brand new because You can allow me to be new sighted.
By this I mean that I can see what I have never seen
before in the old You previously gave me.

Lord, it is the same way You made me new. I just
need to have a Kingdom perspective.
My old has equity and legacy and doesn't have
to cost everything that it's worth.
I have learned that just because something is still
doesn't mean that You are not moving.
Father, my mind was stuck on looking; however,
looking and seeing are not the same.

Thank You for the man of God who has his ear to Your lips.
He can then get all that You have to give to Your people.
I am blessed with new sight.

Dark Shadows

Sometimes there are dark shadows around the recesses of my
mind Lord. I know it is only the enemy trying to take control.
You have given us the ability to shut down whatever he tries
to bring our way because he doesn't mean us any good.
I have the power to turn away from anything
that is not of You and Lord I thank You.

Whenever You show up darkness has to flee. This means if my
mind is on You those shadows have to leave because You are light.
Father, we can't always help what pops into our minds,
but we do have authority over what stays.
Your Word says if we resist the devil, he will flee.
It is to our advantage to oppose every move he makes toward us.

One thing is certain, You did not leave us defenseless.
You are our strong tower and You are only a prayer
away. You are God who hears and answers prayer.
Lord, I bring everything to You, even my
mind, You can work all things out.

Nice but Nasty

There are some people who look nice, they seem to put
on everything that would give them the appearance
of being nice but they treat you nasty.
They have pleasant faces, nice smiles, extended hands,
but their actions show you something else.
It seems they want to befriend you, however, Satan
always raises his head up. We have to keep in mind
that he's prideful so he has to show himself.
Nevertheless, these people attempt to seduce you into trusting them.

Lord, don't they know that we see them for who they really are.
I have learned when people show you who they are, believe them.
I call these people "nice but nasty".
I try to get along with all people, but I
don't get involved with everyone.
My trust is in You leading and guiding me about
all things, even people I associate with.

I pray about things I can't change and that includes people.
I take everything to the altar and leave it there.

Transformed Mind

Some things take place in a life that are beyond explanation.
One of those things is a transformed mind.
When I was born again, it seems that everything about me changed.
No longer did I think about things in the same
way, my perception was different.
My desires were no longer the same; all I wanted was more of You.
What I used to consider dull and humdrum was now a pleasure.
I'm speaking about resting in Your arms.

There was a time when I always had to be into something,
going somewhere, doing something, but then I found You.
I have come to know that spending time with You, reading
Your Word and meditating on it is absolutely wonderful.
It is during these times that I can hear from You.

Father, thank you for peace and joy that the world
didn't give to me and the world can't take away.

Urgent Care

Where do I go when there is no strong foundation for what
I'm going through? The song says "I go to the Rock."
Lord, You are that Rock.
There are times when I need You immediately, I don't always have
time to form a lengthy prayer. All I can do is call Your name.
Those are my urgent care situations.

The blessing is You always show up right on time.
It doesn't matter what things look like or how I feel.
You are concerned and You take care of me.
What may not seem like an emergency to one person
can be a life and death plight for someone else.
It doesn't matter to You because You know everything
pertaining to it and to us. You are omniscient and omnipotent;
additionally, You are everywhere at the same time.

I don't need to explain anything to You. I can just
call You and be assured that You already know
and You are already working things out.
Father You are a right now God, so urgent
care is just a byproduct for You.
I glorify Your name, not for what You can do, simply for who You are.

Fully Saturated

I am fully saturated in You Lord. All of me is
wrapped up and tangled up in You.
I don't want to be left to myself nor is it independence I'm looking for.
You are everything to me Father, even my daily meal.
With You there are no deficiencies because
You are more than enough.

Just knowing that Jesus died for my sins: past, present
and future is more than enough to make me know
there is nothing I can do to repay my debt.
I don't deserve the grace and mercy You give me
every morning and yet You give anyway.
You see all of me, even the parts I don't display. You are well
acquainted with me, and still You pour out Your love.

How can I not serve You? You are pass finding out! You are my God!

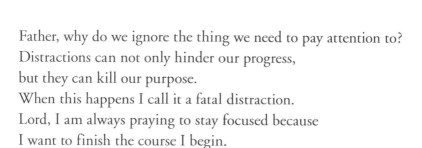

Fatal Distraction

Father, why do we ignore the thing we need to pay attention to?
Distractions can not only hinder our progress,
but they can kill our purpose.
When this happens I call it a fatal distraction.
Lord, I am always praying to stay focused because
I want to finish the course I begin.

I know that the enemy is always working against me. He might
put a stumbling block in my way to stop me in my tracks.
If I allow him to have his way, he will succeed.
But I know that I already have the victory so I keep on keeping on.
Lord, it is Your strength in my weakness that helps me move forward.

A fatal distraction can cause me to abort everything
that you wanted to birth through me.
I can't afford to allow that to happen because
I have a kingdom assignment.
It's not about me, it's all about You.
I want to do the work You've given me to
do, so I just step out on faith.

Shut-In

I remember attending shut-in services. This is when we
spent the night at church. We were truly shut-in with You.
We heard the Word, sang and prayed all night long.
Today, people are too busy doing their own
thing to stop and do Your thing.
I wonder how they think Heaven will be.
Everyday will be Sunday and the Sabbath will have no end.

Lord, we still need to be shut-in. We need
to recognize You as our priority.
We can be shut-in at home, just make a decision
to spend quality time with You.
Turn off the noise and listen as You speak to our hearts.
You desire a relationship with us, and every
relationship needs some alone time.

We need to cultivate our relationship.
We need to come closer and go deeper in You.
Our shut-in doesn't have to be all night
It can just be the allotted time we set for You only.
Everybody can't do it the same, but give us the mind
to do it in our own way, consistently everyday.

Go Fishing

Lord God, if we would do what You said, we would
just go fishing. Sheep begat sheep, so it's our duty to go
out into the world to get others to come to You.
In Your word You gave us the great commission that essentially
tells us to go and teach all nations, baptize them, and
teach them to observe what You have commanded us.
However, we stay in the church and talk with one another.

Some of us never leave the four walls, not
even to go out into the community.
Father, help us to recognize that being
disobedient to Your word is actually sin.
Sin doesn't only consist of what we do; but also what we don't do.
When we don't do what you ask of us we
are leaving our work undone.

Many of us don't realize that we were created
for Your purpose, not for ourselves.
You work through people. We are Your hands and feet.
You gave us the abilities to accomplish everything You
wanted done, but sometimes we just sit down on You.
Your Word tells us that obedience is better than sacrifice

Lord please open our eyes to our faults and
let us be about Your business.
If we look around, we can see that time is running out, and we
have missed so many opportunities to be a witness for You.
Since we don't know when You'll return we need
to make sure our work is finished.
We need to get in a hurry to go fishing.

Second Thoughts

I wonder sometimes if You ever have second thoughts. I know
that You are all knowing and You do things right the first time.
I also know there is no failure in You, so I guess
I'm really thinking about myself.
Lord, I may think that I have made a right
decision, but doubt seeps in.
Doubt isn't a bad thing. It just means I'm not absolutely sure.

Just because everything seems to be okay and nothing
appears to be out of place to me, is it right?
Maybe the better question would be is it Your will?
I prayed beforehand, but did I wait for Your answer or
did I go with the answer I wanted You to give?

Why am I revisiting my actions? I'm not
sad, I don't feel bad, just different.
Sometimes when we come out of our comfort zones we may
second guess ourselves. This could cause second thoughts.
I don't really know the answer, but I know that You do.
Speak to me Lord!

Holy Hush

There are times when we really need to hear from You; times when
we need to sit tight until You make Your wishes known to us.
It is during these times that we must eliminate all
outside distractions and concentrate on You only.
We are so inundated with different noises that they have become a
part of us; so much so, that we hardly seem to notice them at all.
It is absolutely necessary to turn everything off.

Lord, some of us have a hard time getting rid
of the things that cause disturbances.
The first thing we must do is go to a place
where we can be alone with You.
We must turn off the cell phone, it's not really our life line; You are.
We have to get quiet. People, the telephone, television and radio must
not be able to interrupt this time we have designated to be with You.

In my reading, a preacher called this time a "Holy hush".
How appropriate. Wherever we are expecting to meet
with You is a Holy place and we need to wait to hear Your
still, small voice give us life altering instruction.
I believe the enemy uses noise to try to drown You
out, but we must always be aware of his tactics.

Father, thank You for speaking to us. When we read
Your Word, You tell us to meditate day and night.
Meditation requires us to be quiet.
I praise You for bringing scripture to mind when we need it.
Help us to prepare ourselves for a Holy Hush so
that we can hear all You have to say to us.

Right Now

Lord, why do we seem to dwell on the past or plan for
the future without having any regard for right now?
We seem to forget that "now" is all we have. The past
is gone and the future is not promised to us.
Help me to stop putting off for tomorrow what I can do today.

It seems that we take "now" for granted, thinking
that we are supposed to be in this span of time.
We treat "now" as some sort of afterthought
or maybe give it no thought at all.
It is your grace and mercy that allows us to be here.
We didn't wake ourselves up this morning.
We need to recognize how blessed we really are.

Sometimes we think back to what could have,
should have, or would have been.
Never recognizing that those things were never in the plan for us.
You gave us NOW and we can do a lot with that.
We can begin to put Your plans into motion. We must recognize
that You will always do Your part, but we have a part to do as well.

Great things begin with one step. We can't sit and
reminisce, we have to act and we have to do it now.

Inconvenient Love

How fortunate we are to have the love of God. Father,
we really can't fathom how deep Your love is for us.
You don't just love us when we are loving You.
You love us when we turn away.
Your love doesn't manifest itself when we do good. Your
love is evident when we're in our worst state.
You love us in spite of ourselves.

There is absolutely nothing we can do that is
so bad that You refuse to forgive us.
Unforgiveness is not who You are. You are a forgiving God.
You offer an inconvenient love. Your love is not
predicated on circumstances or actions, it's simply
unconditional, no strings attached.
You are love.

Your love is the epitome of what each of
us should be striving to obtain.
You have demonstrated how we are to love one
another, there is no greater love than Yours.
Lord, thank You for loving us with a love that doesn't end.
Thank You for loving us to life.

Rapture Ready

There is nothing else that needs to happen
before You come for Your church.
This lets us know that it behooves each of us to be
rapture ready. We don't know the day or the hour You
will comeback, we just know that You are coming.
Being rapture ready is not about religion or
denomination. You said "be ye holy for I am holy."
Father, on that day we won't have time to
get ready so we better do it now.

I can recall a conversation when a woman said
holiness was for those back then.
She said we can't live holy.
Father she didn't know that You don't expect us
to do the impossible. That's Your job.
However, we can do all things through Christ who strengthens us.
Father, how many others think the same way she does?

When we look at the changes in the world we
can hardly see where morality fits in.
It seems as if everything is acceptable and lawful.
Father, do people understand that when man's law is
contrary to Your will that man's law is wrong.
Nothing supersedes You.
Somehow we have been misguided into thinking
that all the power belongs to us.

Lord, I pray that eyes will be opened and hearts yielded to
You because The Rapture will come sooner than we think.

Internal Medicine

When something is physically wrong on the inside
of me, I go to my internist to get checked out.
Likewise, I need to be examined spiritually as well.
During this spiritual exam I get in position to
receive my internal medicine from You.
I start on my knees giving You praise and glory.

I may stay on my knees or get prostrate when
I really need to stretch out on You.
Not only do I speak, but the Holy Spirit speaks as well.
It's not just talking, but I must listen also to
hear what You have to say to me.
It is during this time that You will tell me about me.

You love me so much that You may chastise me.
You don't allow me to stay in my mess.
You let me know where I have fallen short. Best
of all, You tell me how to correct it.
Lord, just like the loving Father that You are, You soothe my soul.
You continue to pour out Your unconditional
love to me in spite of me.
I am forever thankful to serve such an awe-inspiring God.

Prepared Vessel

In the natural when we have been given an
assignment we want to be prepared.
It is the same in the spirit.
You have given each of us an assignment, it is called purpose.
We are vessels carrying our purposes within ourselves.

Our purpose isn't just for us, it is for the body of Christ
and we want to give the best that we have.
To that end, we must exercise it often so that over time it is perfected.
The saying "if you don't use it you lose it" is true.
Father, You desire that we walk in our calling or
purpose; You gave it to us to be used

I desire to be a prepared vessel so I want to
exercise my purpose as often as I can.
When I first became aware of my purpose, I thought there was
only one way to use it, now I recognize various ways to exercise.
Thank You for letting me see the doors that are open to me.
Father, I must live beyond myself and love beyond
my preferences so that people can see You.

Love must be put into action, not only should
it be seen, it should also be felt.
Talk is cheap, and people get into the habit of saying "I love you" all
of the time; however, real love is evident by how we treat one another.
People will always remember how we make
them feel, not necessarily what we said.
Lord, I want the life I live and the service I give to speak for me.
I don't want to choose certain times or places to demonstrate love
to others. I want to be about love at all times to all people.

Continue to work within me so that this
vessel is prepared to serve You well.

Just Enough

Some things are puzzling to me Lord, so I
come to You for understanding.
I wonder why we believe that just enough is all we should
have when Your Word says that You will pour out a
blessing we won't have room enough to receive.
I know that You are a God of abundance because
You bless us to be a blessing to others.
You give so that we are able to give as well.

Of course, contentment plays a great part, but generally speaking,
so many of us don't realize that if we study Your Word, we
will see that the more we give, the more You give to us.
We can't beat You in giving; but we have to do our part.
Lord, we need to understand that we will reap what we sow, but we
also must comprehend to whom much is given, much is required.

Father, I just want to thank you for overflowing blessings.
Your Word gives us the process by which we will
receive and it says if we bring all the tithes into the
storehouse there will be meat in our house.
This lets us know that giving tithes is not a
suggestion, but it is part of our service to You.
When we obey, You will open the windows of heaven
so that we will be drenched in your blessings.

If only we would be compliant, we wouldn't
have to settle for just enough.
Your Word says eye hath not seen, nor ear heard, neither
have entered into the heart of man, the things which
God hath prepared for them that love Him.

Lord You have already prepared more for
us than we can think to ask for.
If we love You we should be obedient because
obedience is better than sacrifice.

Passed By

We see how others are moving forward and
progressing and wonder why we are passed by.
You operate in seasons, and it might not be our season yet.
Don't allow us to get bitter about someone else's
success; we should celebrate with them.
Ignite a spirit of encouragement within us.
Not only would we be encouraging others, but
we would encourage ourselves as well.

We must remember that we walk by faith and not by sight.
So we must know that what we see is not all there is.
It is a blessing to know that what You do for one You will do for all.
You are not a respecter of persons.
You are God who is all-seeing and all-
knowing. You will bless as You see fit.

Teach us how to wait for our time to come.
Waiting is not the problem, it is what we do
while we wait that makes the difference.
Things may not come when we want them
to, but You have perfect timing.
Help us to know that we haven't been passed by just placed on hold.

Mayday Moment

Mayday is a procedure word used internationally as a
distress signal. It is primarily used in radio communications
by ships and aircraft in life threatening situations.
There are times when we also need a mayday moment.
Your Word tells us to confess our faults one to another,
but we don't always comply; usually we pray to You.

Prayer is great, but you specifically told us to
confess our faults to one another.
You had a reason for that.
We may not always understand, but we don't have to because Your
ways are not our ways, neither are Your thoughts our thoughts.

People have a tendency to lift other people
up instead of lifting You up.
Maybe if we prayed for the frailties in one another, we
wouldn't think more of ourselves than we ought to.
Maybe then we would be obedient to the Word and lift
You up so You would draw people to Yourself.

Lord, remove that proud spirit from us that makes us hide our flaws.
None of us is perfect. We all need to work
on different areas in our lives.
Give us the courage to admit that we need
others to intercede on our behalf.
It doesn't make us weak, it makes us stronger.
A weak man hides and remains the same; a
strong man asks for help and overcomes.

Open Possibilities

Lord, You have poured out so many blessings upon us.
You have even given us open possibilities to pursue.
Open possibilities are the same as doors You open to us, allowing
us to explore the many opportunities that avail themselves to us.
Too often we don't step forward because we are afraid of failure.
We doubt ourselves so much that we don't even try.

We need to realize that failure is one of the steps toward success.
It is something we can learn from.
Father speak to our hearts to move us to action.
Help us to see in ourselves the same things You see in us.
Let us realize that an opportunity means that the
door hasn't already been shut in our faces.

I pray that we stop being doubtful about what we haven't tried.
It's better to make an attempt at doing
something than to only think about it.
We need to shift from ambiguity to trusting in you. Your Word tells
us that we can do all things through Jesus Christ that strengthens us.
It says all things not some things.

I believe we are pregnant with so many possibilities,
but it's up to us to give birth to them.
Having a relationship with You has taught me to look at what You've
already given me instead of complaining about my shortcomings.
When I do this I am able to see that I really
have all I need to move forward.

No Escaping

Lord, I often think about how much You love us.
You are concerned about every inch of us; nothing
is too small or too large for You to notice.
We, tend to dismiss some matters because we
think You don't want to know about them.
Could it be that we forget that You're the same God
who knows the number of hairs on our heads.
You are our Father and there is no escaping anything that
concerns us; nothing is so small that it would go unnoticed
or so large that You wouldn't want to be involved in it.

You are Lord of the ordinary as well as the extraordinary,
so we need to recognize that our everyday affairs are just as
important to You as things that happen once in a lifetime.
Everything that is a concern to us also concerns You.
We don't have to wait until something happens to talk with You. Your
word tells us to pray without ceasing and praying is talking with You.
Throughout the day we can talk with You about
everything that is going on with us.

Lord, I'm so grateful for the opportunity to pray because
all people don't have the same freedom that we have.
I don't want to take anything for granted, because
when I look around, I know I could be in a different
place. It is by Your grace that I am still here.
I understand that You want to hear from me and I have a
listening ear and open heart to receive from You as well.

Not Enough

We should pay more attention to what we say, because
we are usually complaining about not enough.
It seems that we never talk about what is adequate in our
lives, but we're quick to point out what we lack.
Father, I pray that at some point we realize we
should be content with what we have.
You have already given us everything we need to be whole.

When we serve a mighty God all we have to
do is bring our not enough to You.
You, on the other hand, know whether we can handle more or not.
After all, You are the one who made everything out of nothing.
Lord, we must realize that not enough is a spirit
Where is our faith? What kind of witnesses are we? We're not lifting
You up when we don't believe you will do just what You say.

Lord help us to see that people are not only watching
us, they are listening to our complaints.
When we come in contact with others, we are quick
to say that we are blessed and highly favored.
But what we're really doing is being hypocritical,
because we don't believe it ourselves.
However, we really are blessed and we really are highly favored.
We are a royal priesthood and we should start living like it.

Held Back

Oh, how my soul rejoices when I think of how You have
held back things that could have destroyed me.
Lord, You have held back disease and sickness from
overtaking my body. I have been able to take care of
myself, to physically get around, and to help others.
It doesn't have anything to do with what I have or have not
done. It is only by your grace that You decided to hold back.

Father, You have held back natural disasters. I have looked
at the news and seen houses floating along streets. I
have seen wild fires consuming entire communities and
tsunamis overtaking villages and hundreds of people, but
these things did not come near me. You held back.

I could have lost my mind when sudden death
claimed family members, but You held back.

You held back when a truck hit my car on the beltway and my car
was totaled and yet, my daughter and I walked away unharmed.

Father You have held back so many situations and circumstances
that could have altered my life drastically. You looked at
my future and placed me where You wanted me to be in
order to receive the blessings You had in store for me.

You are and have always been in control. Not only is the
beginning of a thing in Your sight, so is the end.

You are the author and finisher of my faith.

Stifled Praise

Stifled Praise….what is it? There is no way a praise can be stifled.
We can't keep our mouths closed when we need to lift You up.
We can't hold our heads down when we need
to look up and give You glory.
Your Word says let everything that has breath praise the Lord.

Lord I praise You with all that is within me.
I will not have rocks crying out in my place
when I have so much to thank You for.
I have to praise You because of who You are.
You are the first and the last, the alpha and the omega.
You are more than enough, a bridge over troubled water.
Lord, You are the solid rock on which I stand.
You are my redeemer, my strong tower, my
protector and my way out of no way.

Just knowing that You have forgiven me for my sins and that
You love me in spite of me causes me to give You praise.
I can't stifle it. I want everybody to know that I serve a risen Savior.
That's something worth talking about.

Surprise Ending

You called us to be Holy because You are Holy. You
also said that obedience is better than sacrifice.
This lets us know that You expect us to strive
to be like You and to obey Your Word.
There will be times when we fall and come
short, it is then that we should repent.
You are a forgiving God. Nothing is so bad
that You will not forgive us.

Some of us have the problem of pretending to be what we are not.
We look like we're walking the walk and we have managed
to get the talk right, but our lives are really in a shamble.
Outside of the church walls and certain
people, we are living like the world.
We can't fool You because You see everything,
there is nothing hidden from You.
We are only fooling ourselves.

Some say they want to enjoy life and don't believe they
need to give up everything they have always enjoyed.
That is because the world we currently live in
urges everyone to live and let live.
Those things that You said were an abomination have now
become legal and some Christians have joined in with the hype.

Father, Your Word said all things are lawful, but not
expedient meaning they are not helpful to us.
You have given us liberty, but liberty does have limitations.
We must be mindful of who we are in Christ
and who we represent in the world.
Otherwise, when this life is over many of
us will have a surprise ending.

Instant Obedience

Instant obedience is the only kind of obedience there is. When
we delay doing what should be done it is disobedience.
Delay is actually procrastination and
procrastination is an opportunity killer.
Procrastination believes there is time; however
opportunity operates on a timeclock.
When You speak to us we should instantly do what You tell us to do.
We must be mindful that You don't operate on
our time, we must operate in Your timing.

When we decide to move in postponed obedience, we
don't receive the full blessing You intended to give us.
Our postponed obedience is only a portion of what
we could have done had we moved instantly.
Lord, open our eyes to the fact that You are all knowing,
so You know exactly what is best for us.

We should be overjoyed that You are ordering our steps.
It is sheer madness to defer Your direction to a
time that seems more convenient for us.
Lord help us to realize that we rob ourselves when we procrastinate
After all we want everything that You have for us.

Seasoning Salt

Father, You created us for Yourself and Your Word
lets us know that we are peculiar people.
There is a difference in us and it should be evident to the world.
We are the ones who should be walking in Your ways
and striving to become more like You daily.
We are the bold ones who aren't afraid to lift You up.

Lord You liken us to salt. We should be seasoning salt. The fact
that we are in this world should make it more palatable.
That's one of the attributes of salt. Not only does it
preserve, but it also makes food taste better.
Our being in the midst of the world should make a difference.

Sometimes, in these latter days, it is hard to see who the
Christians are because we seem to blend in with the world.
There is no demarcation indicating that we
are not the same as the world.
You have us here on earth only for a lifetime,
then You will bring us home to Yourself.
Death of this natural body is not the end, it is
the beginning of eternal life with You.
Earth is not our home. We're just passing through.

Help us to remember You have prepared a
home for us not made by hands.

Sinking Sand

Whenever we stand on anything other than the Solid
Rock which is Jesus, we stand on sinking sand.
We cannot put trust in any other thing to hold us up
against all odds except the God of our Salvation.
People sometimes get things twisted when they
decide to go with man's word rather than believing
every word that proceeds from You Lord.

People can't see any further than their noses at times. They are
so sure that what they have been told is the gospel truth.
It doesn't always matter who they heard it
from, the fact is they believe it.
The real issue is they have put their faith in man
rather than putting their faith in You.
Your Word says to study to show ourselves approved unto
You. This means that if we study the Bible we will be able
to rightly divide the Word for ourselves. We wouldn't have
to quote the misinformation that someone else gives us.

Lord, we must start to hunger for the Word enough to search
it for ourselves. Until we do, we will be like children, tossed
to and fro, and carried about with every wind of doctrine.
In other words, we will be easily deceived.
We must stand on Christ the Solid Rock,
all other ground is sinking sand.

Spiritual Instinct

Your Word tells us not to be anxious about anything (in other words, don't worry), but in everything, by prayer and petition, with thanksgiving, present your requests to God.

We shouldn't find ourselves wide awake at night wondering how to get through a situation, what to do about a circumstance, where the money is coming from or even if we can do what we have been called to do. All of that is worry

We should bring all of these things to you and watch You work it out. Father, we need to develop spiritual instinct. That's when at the inkling of something we can't handle, we turn it over to You. It is when we have that talk with You automatically about everything that concerns us.

It is when we recognize that You should be involved in every part of our lives, the big stuff and the trivial things. We should live a life inclusive with You, not excluding You from any part of it.

Spiritual instinct comes naturally, it's not something we have to think about. It's like breathing, we just do it. You are in us, how can we leave You out of anything that we are in?

New Beginning

You have shown me that even when I've come to the
end of the road I can still begin again. Hallelujah!
Neither my past situation, nor my current
age dictate what You have in store
for me.
Things are not always what they seem; my
eyes may not see a new beginning.
You, on the other hand, will allow it to manifest itself in due season.

You are an all seeing and an all knowing God.
You look at and listen to what my heart says even
when my mind tries to convince me otherwise.
I decided that I would never love again. However, I am
not the one who makes the decisions; You are.

Lord, thank You for a new beginning.
All that I previously had was good because You gave it to me.
Although that love can't be replaced, You've allowed me to add
more love to my life experience, and for that I'm grateful.

Father, I rejoice because You have given me
someone I am equally yoked with.
Someone who puts You first and also loves me in spite of my flaws.
Thank You for letting our latter days be wonderful and
our former days be filled with loving memories.
Lord, thank You for a new beginning.